Waterman's Boy

Susan Sharpe

Waterman's Boy

SILVER BURDETT GINN

Needham, MA   Parsippany, NJ
Atlanta, GA   Deerfield, IL   Irving, TX
Santa Clara, CA

I am grateful to Rod A. Coggin of the Chesapeake Bay
Foundation, who kindly advised me on some errors of
natural history in the manuscript, and to Captain Jackie
McCready and his mate, Nancy Roth, also of CBF, who
generously took me out for a day of water sampling. To
Sharon Steinhoff, my editor at Bradbury Press, thanks in
a hundred ways.

SILVER BURDETT GINN
A Division of Simon & Schuster
160 Gould Street
Needham Heights, MA 02194–2310

Copyright © 1990 by Susan Sharpe
Cover illustration copyright © 1990 by Ondre Pettingill
Glossary © 1996 by Silver Burdett Ginn Inc.
All rights reserved
Published by Simon & Schuster, Elementary Division,
by arrangement with Macmillan Publishing Company
and Ondre Pettingill.

The text of this book is set in 14 point Gael. Book design by Cathy Bobak

Simon & Schuster edition, 1996

1 2 3 4 5 6 7 8 9 10 BA 01 00 99 98 97 96 95

ISBN 0–663–59275–5

To Maitland

1

At four in the morning, Ben heard a chair scrape and knew that his father had already risen for the day's work. Ben lay under the warm covers, listening, his eyes still tight shut. He could smell the coffee that Duke Warren would soon be putting into his thermos.

Ben was not allowed to get up yet. His

mother said a growing boy needed his rest. At seven-thirty he could get up, but then he had to start changing bed sheets and serving breakfast. Last year, when they bought the big house, his mother had opened a bed-and-breakfast. Now tourists visiting Marsh Harbor came to spend the night at the Warren house. Ben was glad about his mother's business, in a way, because tourists paid good money. At least, that's what his mother said. But he did not like helping his mother. He wanted to help his dad, a waterman on the Chesapeake Bay.

Ben opened his eyes a crack. Still dark. Reaching out, he got the clock from beside his bed and held it close to his face. Four-fifteen. Nearly an hour till good light. Ben tried to turn over and be grateful for the warmth of his bed. It didn't work. His fingers and toes tingled, and his head wouldn't stay on the pillow. It was funny how he was only itchy to get up when school was out.

The door latch clicked downstairs and Ben heard the *tap-tap* of his father's footsteps grow fainter. In his mind he saw Duke Warren's big, sturdy body walking down the street, past the sleeping houses, and arriving at the dock. He saw the bare bulbs shining brightly in the crab shanties, heard his father give a quiet good morning to the other men. Finally, he would start the little outboard that would take him to the *Mary*, whose low, white hull could just be seen in the dim light. As soon as his father was finished counting crab pots, stowing his lunch, and turning on the running lights, he would start *Mary*'s engine. Ben thought that he could hear that low watery rumble, away off on the bay. Duke Warren would be the first man out of Marsh Harbor this June morning. He nearly always was.

Ben remembered the feel of the *Mary* on the water, the trembling of the wooden boards under his bare feet as the old diesel engine vibrated. Each summer, for one day, Ben joined his father on the *Mary.* It was a tradition—ever since Ben was six years old. Now he was almost eleven, time enough, he thought, to be a real help.

When he grew up, Ben wanted to be a waterman, like his father. He would never let his parents send him to college, like his older brother, Eddie. Snuggling under his blankets, Ben thought of the crabs, hundreds of greeny-blue, spidery crabs, pouring all over the deck of the *Mary.* In his imagination, he was lifting them up, checking their undersides, throwing them into baskets. Here's a big jimmy, there's a small sook. Here's a big sook, there's a small jimmy. Here's a big . . .

* * *

"Beeen-jy! Seven-thirty. Mom says the people in room four are gone and she needs the room by nine."

"Fix it yourself," he mumbled, but his big sister, Barbara, had already retreated

4

down the back stairs to the kitchen.

Slowly Ben got out of bed and pulled on his jeans from yesterday and a clean T-shirt. He clattered down the back stairs after his sister, and into the aroma of coffee, toast, and biscuits.

In the winter, bed-and-breakfast business was pretty slow—except for holiday weekends—and often the Warrens' guest rooms were completely empty. But in April tourists began to trickle in by twos and threes, staying overnight to take advantage of Marsh Harbor's spring fishing and to give themselves a weekend break from city life. In August, in the heat, business fell off again. But right now, at the end of June, the Warren house was full. This meant cooking breakfast for a dozen people.

Mrs. Warren had chosen the big house for her new business in part because of the huge kitchen that ran all along the back. In the middle of that room was a sturdy wooden table, where today

Barbara was mixing biscuit dough. Morning sunshine beamed onto the table through two long windows with lace curtains. As Ben stumbled into the room, his mother smiled at him, her hair falling gently around her face, like honey on a warm biscuit. Mrs. Warren liked to cook, and that was fine with Ben because he liked to eat.

"You making blueberry muffins this morning, Ma?"

"I ran out of blueberries. I got corn muffins this morning, Ben. Hurry up and eat and you can take the next tray in."

Ben grabbed a couple of pieces of bacon from the microwave and a warm corn muffin. He stood at the window to eat, looking out over the backyard and the rickety picket fence to the backyard of his friend Matt's. Matt's yard was full of interesting things. There was a tire swing, an old Ford truck that didn't run anymore, and Matt's jerry-rigged rabbit hutch that didn't have any rabbits. Matt always said he was going to catch one, but everyone knows you can't catch a rabbit. Harebrained, Matt's mother called him.

Ben and Matt had been friends since before they could remember. So when Grandpa Marsh died two years ago, and Ben's mother had traded in the boat and the property at the edge of town for the big house right behind Matt's, Ben couldn't believe his good fortune. Of course, he was sad about Grandpa Marsh, who had always lived with Ben's family. Grandpa Marsh had been a waterman, too. Plus he carved wooden duck decoys. He could make an old hunk of wood look exactly like a pintail duck, down to the tiny lines in the feathers. Mrs. Warren kept three of his best ones in the front room that was reserved for guests.

Now that Ben and Matt lived so close, they always had some project going. At the moment, they were working on the little skiff they had found abandoned down at the bottom of End Street. Soon they would be able to go crabbing them-selves.

"Wonder how Dad's doing?" Ben said aloud.

"He'll take care of himself, God will-ing," his mother replied. "I hear some new folks in the dining room. You go on in and ask what they want."

Ben stuffed the last of the corn muffin in his mouth and wiped his fingers on his pants. He hated taking the orders. People always asked him how old he was and what he wanted to be when he grew up. And besides, he forgot what they wanted.

"Let Barbara go."

"She's got to get that batch of dough through the processor. Hurry along now, sweetheart."

Barbara held up her floury fingers and made a face at Ben. She had painted her fingernails red. "Gross," said Ben, and went into the dining room. He saw the couple without food and stood in front of them with his hands in his pockets.

"Coffee or tea or hot chocolate?" He began to recite his list.

"Why, thank you. A cup of coffee would be lovely."

"For me, too. With cream."

"Orange or tomato juice?"

The pair thought that over for a few seconds, which was ridiculous, because everybody always said orange. Sure enough, "Orange" they both said together.

"We have bacon, sausage and scrambled eggs, and corn muffins."

When they had selected from these, the woman asked, "Are you going to be a waiter when you grow up?"

"No," answered Ben.

"I'll bet he wants to be a fireman," said the man.

Hastily Ben scooted toward the kitchen.

After all the guests had been served, it was time to clean the rooms. There were seven guest bedrooms up and down the long hall that ran from the front to the back of the Warren house. Mrs. Warren had had each of the big old bedrooms divided in half, and a toilet and shower put at the back of each one. The last space, which could have been room eight, was a bathroom for Ben and his family. Their bedrooms were at the back, over the kitchen. At least they didn't need clean sheets every day. Ben didn't see why, if guests stayed for only one night, they couldn't leave the sheets for the next people in that room. But when he had suggested this plan, his mother and Barbara only laughed at him.

Ben thought Barbara should do all the rooms, because she was a girl. Or maybe Mrs. Jamison, who sometimes worked for his mother. But Duke Warren said Ben should help out. And, Ben reasoned, if he were good and obedient, maybe his father would change his mind about sending him to college.

In room four, he set about the regular

routine: gathering up the towels (even the ones that looked like they hadn't been used), dusting the dresser tops and the bedside tables. Then he pulled back the covers and tugged at the sheets on the big double bed. One corner wouldn't come. Ben tugged again, and there was a little ripping sound. Uh-oh. He went around to the other side where he could pull from a different direction and gave a bigger tug. *Rrrr-ip!* Holding up the sheet, Ben saw a gash in the corner where it had caught on a bedspring. He put the torn sheet in the big laundry hamper by the phone in the hall and went on with the job, fuming now. How was he supposed to know the dang sheet was hooked?

The people had left a fishing bobber in the top drawer, and Ben pocketed that. He checked the wastebasket, too, because you never could tell. This one had some candy wrappers but no candy, a sock with a big hole in it, and a piece of paper with a list on it. Ben read it but it wasn't very interesting. It said "Post-cards" at the top and had names checked off underneath. Everyone was checked except Aunt Sally. Ben guessed she didn't get a card.

When he was finished with the room, Mrs. Warren came to inspect Ben's work. She ran her finger along the bed table and pulled back the covers to make sure the sheets were straight and smooth. She gave them an extra tug.

"Good boy, Ben honey. You're getting the smart of it."

Ben made a face at her, feeling guilty about the sheet. Even so, he didn't feel moved to tell her. "Can I go to Matt's now?"

"Yes, Ben, Mrs. Jamison will be here in time to handle the rest. You run along and have fun. Mind you watch the cars when you're on your bike."

Letting the screen door slam, Ben bounded down the porch steps and picked up his rusty blue bike from where it had fallen on the lawn. He hopped on in one smooth motion, and in seconds he was winging around the corner past the Dari Dreme and hanging a left up to Matt's. He forgot to look for traffic when he turned left. Too late, he checked. Nothing was coming.

When Ben arrived, Matt was out in the backyard, picking up pieces of quartz from the edge of the garden. Ben could see the back of his curly blond head.

"Hey, Matt."

"Hey, Ben."

"What are you doing with those rocks?"

"I'm gonna save them. Miss Thompson said a lot of things are going to be scarce in the twenty-first century, things we just take for granted. So I'm gonna save this stuff for about fifty years, and then, when there isn't any more quartz, I'll be rich. You wanna be in on it?"

"But what's quartz good for?"

"It's gonna be real rare."

"Naw, come on, let's go work on the boat."

Matt shrugged and got up from his knees. "I got some caulk," he said.

"Matthew!" called a voice. It was Matt's mother. Holding a basket of laundry, she peered out the back door at Ben. "Where you going?" she asked.

"Just playing," Matt answered.

"What are you doing with that caulk? You boys got yet another harebrained scheme? You're not fooling around with a boat?"

"Maybe," said Matt, swinging up his bicycle and tossing the caulk into the basket.

"I thought so," she said, but she was smiling. "You sure it doesn't belong to anyone?"

"Sure." Matt stood over his bicycle, one foot on the pedal.

"And you know where the deep water is?" his mother cautioned.

"We're just going to that old rowboat, was down in the marsh grass on End Street. We're fixing it up, aren't we, Ben?"

"Yup," said Ben. "We're gonna catch crabs."

"You boys bring me some, then, and don't be late, Matthew. Your father'll be home before five tonight, and we'll eat early because it's town meeting night."

"Okay, Mom." And the boys were off, swinging down to Main Street and over to End where it went down by the water and turned rough over ground-up oyster shells. There lay their boat, nearly hidden by cordgrass, but almost ready to be pushed into the water, just as soon as it was caulked and painted.

2

Ben's arms ached that night from hours spent caulking. His father must have been tired, too, because over dinner he was cranky. He started off on one of his favorite complaints: how the town of Marsh Harbor was changing.

"By April this year, folks were thicker

around here than herring," Duke observed.

And Mary Warren answered, "I'm thinking of putting a wing on the house, Duke, and taking on Mrs. Jamison full-time. I do believe I could fill six more rooms."

The town of Marsh Harbor, Maryland, on the Eastern Shore of the Chesapeake Bay, had one main street. It ran parallel to the water, from the marsh at the north end to the dock at the south end. A half dozen streets sliced Main Street crosswise. Ben's house was on one, Matt's on the next. Marsh Harbor was an old town where, for generations, families had made their living on the water. You could see the old family names in the graveyard: the Marshes, the Warrens, the Fishers, the Thomases, the Smiths. In the summer, making a living on the water meant crabs; in the winter, mostly oysters.

Recently, though, there were changes

in town. Down at the south end there was a marina, where you could rent a boat to take you fishing for a day. Right on Main Street was a new inn, with a deck over-looking the water and a VISA/Mastercard sign in the window. Once Ben and Matt started in the door, just to see, but a door-man said, "Can I help you?" and led them right back outside.

Ben didn't much care about the new buildings and bigger crowds as long as he was allowed to ride his bicycle wherever he wanted and breakfast duty didn't take any longer. He looked forward to having Mrs. Jamison around more. He thought she would be a lot better than he at tak-ing the orders and changing the beds. But that evening, the caulking done, his mind was mostly on painting the boat with Matt.

* * *

The next morning, eager to get out, he scooted toward the kitchen with what he was sure was the last order.

18

"Not so smart there, mate." A man's voice stopped him. "There's one more for morning mess."

At the back corner table was a young man sitting all by himself. Ben thought he was nice-looking, not like a regular tourist, but something else. He went over.

"Orange or tomato?"

"Got any oysters?"

"For *breakfast*?"

"That's what my grandpa used to have. Raw oysters for breakfast. Course, he'd already been out on the water two, three hours by then. Well, scrambled eggs then."

Ben smiled. "Was your grandpa a waterman from around here?"

"Not right here. We lived up near the Nanticoke."

"Did you want to go out with him, when you were a kid?"

"You bet. I wanted it so bad I snuck out of the house one time, slept over on the boat." Ben snickered, and the man went

19

on. "Well, he worked me so hard I never wanted to go again."

Ben's face fell. "You never went again?"

"No, I just never *wanted* to. It's hard work, oystering. Sometimes Grandpa went after crabs, sometimes rockfish, sometimes blues, when they were running. But just about everybody in my family has given up the water."

"Not my dad. My dad's a waterman. He's after crabs right now."

"Crabs." The guest looked thoughtful. "How's he doing?"

"Well . . ." Ben remembered his father's serious talks with his mother, all June. He heard them sometimes at night, when he was supposed to be asleep. "Well, not too good, I guess."

"Ben." He hurried into the kitchen, where his mother was impatiently waiting. "Hurry up now, child. That other couple's been waiting ten minutes. What are you talking with that fella about? It's your job to keep polite and not take up the guests' time. Here, they want muffins? Carry this in. What did he order?"

"Scrambled eggs. But Mom . . . "

He knew it was a lost cause—she was in her morning frenzy. "You finish up in here, Barbara," his mother said. "I've got to go mind the desk. That's the last of the guests for the morning. Ben, soon as you take the eggs in, room three has to be cleaned. I got new people coming in around ten. So get a move on."

When Ben brought the scrambled eggs, the man was studying the tide tables in the paper.

"Going fishing?" asked Ben, setting the plate down.

"Not exactly."

"My friend and me got a boat," said Ben. He couldn't help himself. "Am I bothering you?"

"Not at all. I need company. Are you going fishing?"

"We're going crabbing. When we get

our boat fixed up. We don't have any oars, so we're going to pole it. I saw some older kids doing that, and my brother, Eddie, showed me how. Eddie's at Eastern Shore Community College. I'm not going to college; I'm going to follow the water, like my dad."

"Is that what your dad says?"

Ben paused. "No, my dad wants me to go to college, too. I don't really want to go. School is okay, for when you're a kid, but as soon as I can quit, I am."

The man studied Ben carefully, eyeing his wavy brown hair (like his mother's), thin arms and legs, and soft brown eyes. Recently, Ben wished he had straight black hair like his dad, and those same sharp blue eyes with the thousand dark wrinkles around them from squinting in the sun. But the man at the table, looking at Ben, seemed to like what he saw.

Ben studied the man in turn. He was young and good-looking, sort of like Indiana Jones. He had on neat workman's pants and a blue denim shirt. Ben also noticed that his hands were not sliced up, like a waterman's, or calloused from handling ropes.

"What's your name?" they both asked at the same moment, and laughed.

"Ben Warren."

"David Watchman. How do you do?"

"Well, what are *you* going to do today?"

"Collect plankton."

Ben was silent. Having spent his entire life on the Chesapeake, he thought he had learned about all the birds, all the fish, all the animals, even all the biting insects. But he had never heard of plankton.

"What?"

The man looked at him seriously. "You know my name? David Watchman. That's what I do, I watch the water. Not in the regular way. I take samples in different places. Then I take these to a lab and count the number of microscopic plants and animals in a droplet. This tells me a lot about the health of the water in a particular spot. Around the bay here, there's a team of people like me. We put all our information together, and then—"

"You mean you're a scientist?"

"Yes."

"My grandpa was named Marsh. Grandpa Marsh. And he lived on the marsh, all his life until he died."

"And Sally Ride was an astronaut."

Ben laughed. Then he said, "Ben Warren. That doesn't mean anything."

"It means something. You just haven't discovered what it is yet. You have to put your own meaning into your name."

"Beeen-jy!" Barbara came prancing into the breakfast room, tossing her brown hair ("chestnut," she called it). "Boy," she said to Ben, "are you gonna catch it."

"Oh, is that a fact?" Ben didn't want to talk to his sister in front of his new friend.

24

"Mrs. Jamison's doing the laundry and she found this sheet with a rip in it. She's gonna tell Mom."

"Big deal." Ben glanced at David Watchman. He didn't want to discuss the silly stuff he did every morning.

"Mom'll know who did it."

"Big deal."

Barbara batted her eyes at David Watchman. "We have to help my mother," she explained, drawing herself up tall.

"I see," he said. "Please tell your mother that I ripped my sheet myself, quite accidentally, last night. It must be the one that got to the laundry already. Perhaps she'd be so good as to put it on my bill." And nodding to Ben, he said, "Catch you later, pal," and was gone.

Barbara looked quite embarrassed. "Sorry, Ben," she muttered. "Who *is* that guy, anyway?"

"He's a scientist," Ben replied. "And *you* have to clean up breakfast." Then he flashed a smile and trotted off to room three with a hum on his lips.

* * *

When Ben was finally free that day, he found out that Matt had to mow the lawn for *his* mom. So at two in the afternoon, he went down to the dock to watch for the watermen to come in. Trailing his toes in the water, he contentedly breathed in the smell of fish and gasoline. The water slapped pleasantly against the old gray boards, and the whole dock groaned and squeaked in a slow, easy rhythm. Since it was a nice clear day, warm for sure on the water, Ben knew that the men would have to come in before long so their baskets of crabs wouldn't spoil.

Duke Warren was the third boat in. Ben spotted the *Mary* as soon as it showed on the horizon. He knew the particular lines of the hull and the rumble of the engine, which sometimes skipped a beat. Ben stood to catch the line his father threw, and wrapped it around the post to hold the boat fast. Then his father stepped off the *Mary* and secured the other end.

"Good catch, Dad?"

"We take what the Lord sends us."

That meant no. Ben peered into the boat and counted only seven bushel baskets, one of them not quite full.

"Can't make a living on that," said Duke.

"How come there are so few crabs this summer, Dad?"

"Well, son, you answer that, you'd have a lot of interested watermen around to hear." Duke smiled and shook his head, but all the same, there were little worry lines on his face. "Some say it's the pollution. Some say it's the hard winter. Some say it's the hot summer. Tell you what I say, Ben my boy, I say you follow your brother Eddie to that college so you won't have to worry about the water. Eddie is doing right well."

27

Ben didn't say anything as he followed his dad into the crab shack. Even this small catch had to be sorted and packed into the cardboard boxes that were stacked high all around, with "Fresh Seafood" printed in blue on their sides.

A lot of the crabs in Duke's baskets were peelers. They had a red mark on them which meant they were about to molt. These crabs went into a special floating tank that had fresh sea water flowing through it all the time. In a few days, the peelers would wriggle out of their shells, and then bang, before the new shells could harden, they would be packed as "softshell." Softshell crabs brought more money because people could eat the whole thing without having to pick the meat out of the shell.

Ben felt good, working beside his father. He was careful never to rip or ruin anything. Sometimes he had to hold up a crab that was only partly showing the red mark. "Is this one ready yet?" Then his father would tell him whether to put it in the float or into the boxes. Sometimes Duke Warren would say to the other watermen, "Ben is a good boy, knows his crabs. He doesn't make mistakes." When his father said those words, Ben felt that all was right with the world. How could he ever want to be anything but a good waterman?

"Dad," Ben asked, "what do you think my name means?"

His father looked amused. "Mean? Names don't mean anything. If they did I'd be a Duke. I'd have a castle in England. How would you like that?"

Ben shook his head. "I like it here fine, Dad."

"You help your mother this morning?"

"Yeah. Oh, and Dad, one of the guests is a scientist."

"Umph." Duke Warren frowned at the box he was fastening. "What kind of a scientist?"

"Some kind of a sea scientist. He collects p—. I don't know. Some kind of little stuff that's in the water. He's like, testing it."

"Plankton."

"Yeah, that's it." Ben beamed at his father. "You sure know a lot, Dad."

"Yeah, well, I know a thing or two that might surprise those pointy-headed scientists." Ben took a step back; his father's voice was so angry. "Those are the fellas that go up to Annapolis and tell 'em we can't go out on the water anymore. You know the reason I only go out once a week in winter oystering is because it's the law. I can only go certain places, I can only use certain equipment."

"I know that, Dad."

"And you know I can't provide for the family, the way my father did. Are you hearing me, Ben?"

"Yes, Dad."

"And it's because the government is putting their fool heads in where they don't know what's going on. Why don't

30

they listen to the watermen? Oh no, they get some egghead in there, tells them the problem with the bay is the watermen. My father and my grandfather fished this bay every day of their working lives, except Sunday. Wasn't anything wrong with it then. They're just taking away our income without knowing a fool thing about it." Ben knew his father was no longer really talking to him. He was talking to the specters in the air that so often made him angry. Now Duke Warren pulled too hard at the rope around his box and it broke. He threw it aside and then noticed Ben again.

"Sorry, boy. But I don't want you being friendly with that scientist. We don't want that kind around here. You go off, now. I've got things to do in town. And don't be hanging around here so much," he added, as an afterthought.

"I'm sorry, Dad."

Duke Warren softened. "You're a good boy, Ben. But I don't want you hankering after a life on the water. There's no future in it. You see now, we've got to depend on your mother." He shook his head slowly.

"Mom likes to work, Dad."

"You're right about that, son." And Duke Warren laughed. "Even if you don't like helping *her*. Why don't you run on ahead and let her know I'll be home soon."

So Ben walked slowly home, past the T-shirt shop, the police station, and the drugstore. Old Mr. Smith, the drugstore owner, waved from behind the counter. Ben could remember just a few years ago when Mr. Smith's store had toothpaste and Band-Aids and regular stuff. Now it, too, was stocked for tourists. Fishing tackle and sunscreen filled the front windows, and the owner spent most of his time making submarine sandwiches for people spending the day in charter boats. Thinking of subs made Ben hurry a little faster. He was hungry.

3

Every year, on the Fourth of July, the town of Marsh Harbor held a crab festival. Out of towners would pour in and fill all the guesthouses, the parking spaces, and the shops. The streets were so full then it was best to bicycle, because only bicycles could move. Over at Memorial Park, there was a big picnic, with nothing but the first sweet corn of the year and crabs—crabs by the hundreds, cooked in every possible way. There were crabs steamed in Old Bay seasoning, and crabmeat salads, and softshell crab sandwiches, and crab chowder, and crab mixed with flour and egg and spices to make crabcakes. Every year there was a contest for the best new crab recipe, and this year Mary Warren aimed to win.

Ben and Matt aimed to win the crab race. They had been working feverishly to get their boat painted, so they could catch their crab before the contest.

The racecourse was laid out on a plywood track, ten yards long. Any crab that fell over the edge was disqualified. Once the race started, you weren't allowed to touch your crab, even if he stopped to fight or got sidling in the wrong direction. The prize for the winner was five dollars and a little crab trophy, which you could keep for the rest of your life. The boys hadn't decided how to divide the winnings. Sometimes Ben figured he would keep the five dollars and let Matt have the trophy, but sometimes he thought he'd rather have the trophy. Matt said they could split the money and trade the trophy every week until one of them died and then he would leave it in his will for the other one. Ben wasn't so sure.

On the first of July, the paint was dry on Ben and Matt's boat and it was ready to launch, just in time. The tourists who entered the crab race caught their crabs in the tidal guts, with pieces of chicken neck tied to a string as bait. But Ben and Matt knew that there were even more, even bigger crabs out in the eelgrass, where the water was shallow and the bottom was deep and mucky and smelled of salt and dead things. To catch crabs out there you wanted a nice flat-bottom boat and a big net. With a long pole, you'd push the boat along to a good spot and then you'd float quietly and feel for the big tug on your chicken.

The day of the launch, Mrs. Warren finally settled on something she called Vegetable Crab Soufflé. She served it to Ben for lunch. It sat there on his plate, a mass of eggy stuff with weird vegetables stuck in it. Barbara said, "Oh, Mother, it's just delicious. I'm sure it'll get second prize at least." Ben slipped off his chair and out the door.

* * *

It took both boys working together to push the newly painted boat right side up.

"We ought to give her a name," said Ben.

"I know," said Matt. "I've been thinking. How about *Intrepid Voyager*?"

"That's dumb," said Ben, waving his hand. "Here, chuck your net and pole in."

Their stuff tossed inside, the two boys stood on either side of the skiff. It was high tide, so the boat was only about five feet from the water, sitting on mud and cordgrass.

"One, two, three," said Ben. "Heave!"

They heaved, but the heavy wooden boat would not budge.

"Come on," said Ben, "we're not doing it right. Both of us stand behind, like this. Ready? Okay, one, two, three—"

"Heave!" they both yelled together. The boat moved a couple of inches and stopped.

Matt and Ben scratched their heads. "Got to make a runway for it," Matt decided finally. Ben agreed. So they went around the bow and began tramping down the cordgrass, covering their sneakers and socks with the rich mud. Soon there was a slick, watery pathway in front of the boat. When they heaved together again, this time, inch by inch, they crept toward the little wavelets that seemed to beckon their craft. At last the tip of the bow dipped into the water. One more good push, and they would have her. Ben and Matt looked at one another and grinned. Streaks of mud and sweat had somehow gotten all over them. But who cared?

"One, two, three, heave!" The boat slipped faster as it moved out into the water, and they kept going with it.

"Hurray, we did it!" They jumped up and down and did a little dance.

But when they stopped, their cheering seemed foolish. For there, sunk in five inches of water, was the *Intrepid Voyager.* The boys watched the water gurgling in past the patches and caulk and filling.

Ben thought he was too old to cry, but he was tempted.

"Hey!" hailed a friendly voice. "Need a ride?" It was David Watchman, putting along in his scow.

"Our boat sunk," explained Ben dolefully. If the man had seen the whole thing, he thought, at least he wasn't laughing. "And we have to catch a crab for the fair."

"I've seen some big ones out in the eel-

grass around Little Bit Island," said
David. "Nobody seems to bother with
that spot out there."

"Can't get there without a boat," Matt
replied crossly.

"I'm headed that way," David said.
"Grab your nets there. You get crabs and
I'll get copepods. Have you back here in
an hour. Just don't you boys tip over my
specimens."

Matt looked at Ben. "Who is that guy?"
he whispered.

"He's a scientist. He's staying at my
mother's. He seems okay, but my dad
doesn't care for him much." Ben hesitated, looking at the young man's friendly
face and the boat.

"Did he *say* you weren't allowed to go
out with him?"

"No, he never said that." And without
further hesitation, both boys took seats at
opposite ends of David Watchman's boat.

"Just fasten that around you, good and
snug," said the man, handing them each

a life jacket. Rats, Ben thought. He hated life jackets. You couldn't move your arms properly in them, and this one was so big it rubbed his chin.

"It isn't deep between here and Little Bit," he protested.

"Just put the jacket on." The man's manner was no-nonsense. "We'll anchor over there, and then you can take the jacket off for handling your net."

Ben did as he was told and they headed out. A white egret stood severely on shore, watching them depart. Even in a little outboard, Ben loved to be on the water. Everything seemed to open up around him, making the world twice as big and twice as beautiful, blue and breezy and sparkling. Underneath them a jellyfish floated by, all wavery like hair in a swimming pool.

"What kind of fish did you say you were after?" asked Matt.

"Copepods. It's not a fish. It's a little

crustacean that lives in the water, part of the plankton."

"My father knows about plankton," said Ben.

Matt had more questions. "What are you checking them for?" he asked.

"I'm not exactly checking them; I'm counting them. This is a plankton net." David unwound a curious device, like a jar with a leg of panty hose attached. He threw the jar behind the boat, where it dragged along in the water.

"That's not really panty hose, is it?" asked Ben.

"No, of course not, it's just a very fine net. Water goes through, but it gathers plankton and moves them along back into the jar."

"Wait!" interrupted Matt. "There's crabs down there! Lots of them!"

They had arrived at one end of Little Bit, but David Watchman didn't stop the motor. "That's nothing," he said. "We're going down to the other end."

He took them to a place where the eel-grass underwater was so long and thick you could hardly see through. Little snails and shrimp clung to the waving fronds of grass, and schools of baby fish darted away from the shadow of the boat. Eagerly, the boys threw out their lines with the smelly old pieces of chicken wing on them and readied their nets.

Expertly drawing in his line, Matt landed a six-inch jimmy neatly in the bottom of the boat. "Got one!" he yelled.

"Whoa!" said David. "Watch that box. I can see I've brought the right watermen out here. Did I mention the fee for the use of this boat?"

Ben looked worried for a moment, but the man winked at him.

"I get the two biggest for my own dinner."

"Aw, no, not the biggest! You can have *all* the crabs under six and a half," Ben offered. "See, we're not aiming to eat

these crabs. They're crabs for the race."
And he described the Fourth of July festival.

"I've got to leave town later today to
check out a problem," David said, "but
I'll be back in time to cheer you on. Look
there!"

The man had sharp eyes, all right.
Right off the port side, hanging on to
Ben's chicken wing, was the biggest crab
Ben had ever seen, maybe nine inches
across. Holding his breath, Ben eased the
net around the creature's back, being
careful not to stir the water. Then, quick
as a flash he scooped. The crab was the
loveliest, biggest, greenest jimmy in the
whole northern half of the Chesapeake,
Ben would swear to it. And look at those
bright blue claws!

The boys caught a dozen more before
they quit, but none bigger than Ben's
jimmy. "He's our crab," agreed Matt,
"sure as gun's iron."

Before they left, David pulled in the

plankton net. He held the jar up to the light and looked at it. Then he held up the net itself.

"Anything wrong?" asked Ben, seeing David's frown.

"Just a little something I don't like to see," said David. He showed Ben a few drops of black oil beaded up on the net. He set the net aside with a shrug and headed the boat back toward the dock.

"Could be just some pleasure boat, dumping its oil," said Ben.

"Could be," said David, "could be. That would be against the law, of course. Any way you figure, I don't much like it."

4

The Fourth of July dawned bright and clear. Mary Warren had her family up early, with a houseful to feed and the crab soufflé to prepare. While Ben and his mother ferried breakfast orders, Barbara shut herself in the bathroom. She had a date for the festival with a funny-looking guy named Lennie, who worked at the inn and acted like Ben was invisible. Ben couldn't wait to get over to Matt's. In trial heats in his friend's basement, their crab had proved to be as fast as he was large. The boys felt confident. Matt had already painted "Champ" on the crab's back.

By ten in the morning, Matt and Ben were at the fairgrounds. Firemen were setting up the cannon for the fireworks and marking off the places where folks could sit. Strangers were setting up a small Ferris wheel and some games. A couple of men were at work on the crab course, and a lot of women, maybe twenty, were laying things out on long tables—cloths and dishes and flowers and watermelons—and going in and out of the kitchen of the Methodist church next door.

Ben and Matt were not about to miss a thing. They carefully stowed their champion crab in a box and tucked him in a secret spot in the shade. He was wrapped in wet newspaper with seaweed and a whole chicken neck to eat, so he'd feel good and peppy when he came out for the afternoon race.

The first thing the boys checked out was exactly where the corn was going to be boiled this year. When the corn was ready, you didn't want to have to wait in line half your life to get a piece. Ben and Matt found the spot where Mrs. Mallock had already laid a fire, the same place where it was last year. She had a big, old-fashioned iron tripod with the pot hanging from a chain over the coals.

"You Mary Warren's boy?" she asked, when she saw Ben standing there.

"Yes."

"You take after your daddy. You and your friend there, run and fetch me some water from the kitchen, will you? This kettle holds upwards of ten gallons, and it'll take its sweet time getting to boil. So we may as well get started."

"How come you don't just boil it in the kitchen?" asked Matt. "There's a big, automatic gas cookpot in there."

Mrs. Mallock winked. "Well, we do, of course, honey. This fire out here's for the tourists. They like to think we're fifty years behind."

So Matt and Ben took the gallon milk jugs Mrs. Mallock gave them and lugged them back and forth from the Methodist church next to the park. They had to lift the jugs up to their shoulders to pour them into the kettle, and Ben spilled one, so the task took them quite a while. But it had an unexpected reward. When they were finished, Mrs. Mallock said, "Thank you very much, boys. You come back soon as the corn's ready, hear, and I'll find you some good pieces." They assured her they would and went to check out the midway.

The Octopus was the new ride this year, and Ben and Matt agreed it was pretty good. Except for the Ferris wheel, the rest were pretty tame. And there were the usual games. They tried the one where you threw pennies onto squares and got the prize pictured on that square. It looked easy. But most of the squares just had a balloon and most of the time the pennies landed on lines. The man in the booth wasn't very friendly, either. If your penny was even the least little bit on a line, he just swept it off and put it in his bag. He didn't even look at you or care what you said.

At noon, Matt and Ben returned for the corn. Mrs. Mallock was as good as her word, and fetched them out two huge, golden ears, a little wisp of steam just curling off the ends. Carrying the hot corn with napkins, the boys went to the tables and rolled the ears in butter and salt. It was the first corn of the season, and very sweet. Ben liked it even better than crabcakes or potato salad or blueberry pie, though he did have a large slice of pie even after two ears of corn, a wedge of watermelon, three pickles, and a chocolate cupcake.

Matt ate pretty much the same. He lay back under a tree with a satisfied moan and patted his stomach. "Now I have really run ashore," he said, repeating his father's favorite after-dinner comment.

While the two boys sprawled on the ground together, Barbara strolled by with Lennie.

"That's my little brother," she said, pointing him out to Lennie as if Ben were just an interesting sight in the park. Ben stuck out his tongue after her, but Barbara was being too prissy to notice.

At two o'clock everyone gathered for the crab race. Boys of all ages carefully carried boxes and coolers and bags to the track. Even some grown men were entering the race, and two girls. Ben looked at the containers, wondering about the crabs inside. Then he saw David Watchman, who gave him an encouraging wave.

While the coach from Marsh Harbor High School laid out the rules, each crab got a sticker with a number on it. There were twenty-three crabs in all. Carefully, Matt raised the lid of their cardboard box while Ben stuck the number fourteen onto Champ's back. Champ snapped a claw. That was good. He was rarin' to go.

Next, each starter grabbed hold of his crab from the back and took a place along the starting line. Ben was Champ's starter. He wiggled and pushed until he got a good place right near the middle of the table. There Champ was less likely to fall off.

Next to him was a boy Ben recognized from school. His name was Evan Fisher and he was in the next grade up.

"We've got good spots," said Evan with a grin.

Ben nodded. He looked up and down the line. The crowd was laughing as crabs grabbed for each other in the air. Nowhere did Ben see a crab as big as Champ. He glanced at Matt and signaled A-OK.

"Ready?" called the coach, and the answer "ready" echoed up and down the line.

"On your mark, get set . . . Hey, wait a minute, get that little feller up there." A little boy with a very small crab had set him on the table too soon. The crowd roared again.

"On your mark, get set, GO!" At the sound of a whistle, the crabs hit the table and the battle began. There were loud scraping and cracking noises as crabs scuttled sideways and backward, never forward, grabbing at each other, backing away. Three immediately tumbled off the track, including Evan's. The boy picked him up with a good laugh.

But Champ was doing well. After an initial skirmish with the crab on his right, he made a quick foray to the left and turned ninety degrees, so that when he retreated from the next crab, he was going sideways toward the goal.

"Come on, Champ! Go, Champ!" Ben

and Matt jumped up and down together, screaming. Now Champ charged his rival. He was right in the middle of the thickest of the fray, swinging his claws to right and left, showing off his superior size. One crab had just backed away from him and another had his claw locked when *Tweeet!* the coach's whistle blew. Ben looked up in disbelief.

Someone else had won!

It was the little boy whose crab had started too soon. Ben guessed the kid was hardly out of kindergarten. Now he remembered seeing the boy's crab, backing away from the fight. The runt must have backed and backed himself right over the finish line.

"Dag," said Matt as they watched the boy's father carry him on his shoulders to receive the trophy.

"Too bad it wasn't a battle, instead of a race," said Ben. "Then we would've won for sure."

"Let's let Champ go," Matt suggested,

and Ben agreed. After all, their hero had done his best; he just didn't understand the rules. "Next year, we'll really train one," Ben said.

They put Champ in the water right there at the edge of the park. The second he was free, the crab was off sideways, leaving behind a little wake of mud particles.

Now it was time for Matt to be home, so Ben went off in search of his parents. He wondered how his mother had done in the cooking contest. You never could tell what grown-ups might like.

But he found his father first. Duke Warren was standing with a group of watermen. They were talking in such serious voices that he could not interrupt. He sidled up to his father and listened.

"One day a week," Mr. Thomas was saying. "Going to be the same next winter as it was last. One day a week, they let me go out. Gotta be Tuesday. I told the man, I said to him, 'Look, suppose the tide's not right Tuesday, suppose we got a storm—you're going to have men going out when they shouldn't.' 'Tuesday,' he said to me, like he was some robot. Tuesday." Mr. Thomas spat on the ground, and there was a little respectful silence.

"I reckon we're all in that boat," said another man.

"Government don't know what they're talking about," added Duke Warren. Ben did not like the bitter tone of his father's voice. "Those state boys want to board my boat, I'll give them an earful. Last week I had one of those marine police, stood on my boat for two hours, measured every damn crab I had, and he didn't find any under the size limit. He says, 'I know you got some here, Mr. Warren.' I says, 'You go on using up my good time, I'm not going to have crabs nor pots nor boat. I'm going to be forced off the water, like most of the rest of them.' "

"It doesn't matter how much time you spend," said a man with a green cap. "I been on the water sixty, seventy hours a week. There's not enough crabs in the whole bay to support a dozen watermen this summer."

Duke huffed and shook his head. "There's crabs," he said firmly. "You just got to find 'em."

"I haven't seen *you* coming in loaded down, Duke Warren," replied Green Cap.

Duke looked at the ground. Ben hated to see his father like that, with nothing to say back. He gathered his courage to speak aloud. "There's crabs around Little Bit Island," Ben said.

The men all looked at him and smiled, and then they grinned at Duke. Suddenly Ben was embarrassed. His father motioned for him to say no more and Ben was relieved. He hated to have everyone looking at him. What if he said something wrong?

"It's the same with the rockfish," said the man next to Ben, picking up Green Cap's complaint. "Can't take them at all now. I can remember, when my daddy was young, who-whee, the fish we'd take in a day, you won't see the like now in a week of Tuesdays." There was a nodding and murmuring all around. Everyone remembered better times.

Ben noticed David Watchman standing nearby, not really part of the group, but listening.

"It's been bad before," said someone hopefully. "It comes back. There's rhythms in things. Get the government off our backs, and it'll come back."

"Some folks live on government handouts." It was Mr. Thomas again. "We don't live like that around here. We go our own way. We don't need either help, and we don't need either government to tell us what to do." Again, there was approval all around.

"Yes, you do," said a crisp voice. Everyone looked up in surprise at David Watchman. "You do need help from the government."

A chorus of objections followed. "That's not our way." "Where you from, youngster?" "Man looks like he's from Annapolis himself."

"Name's David Watchman," said the scientist firmly. "I grew up near the Nanticoke." The men relaxed a bit. They respected a man who spoke up for himself, and the Nanticoke was part of their bay and their way of life.

"You've got problems on the bay you can't solve by yourselves," David went on. Ben admired his confident manner. "You know yourselves, better than anyone else, how the harvest is down. Well, there's reasons, and some of those reasons have nothing to do with you. You've got waste coming down from Baltimore and Washington. You've got a lot of suburbanites up the bay who love their lawns and pack them full of fertilizer and then pack them full of pesticides. You've got development everywhere, with bulldozers pushing soil into the water. These all run down into your water and poison your fishing grounds. One person can't solve all these problems alone. We've got to get people from all over the state together on this. We've got to get folks from Virginia and Delaware, too. That's a job for government. And the more you take part, the better off you're going to be."

The men listened attentively to this speech, but some shook their heads and looked doubtful.

"I can't keep food on the table with all their regulations," said one.

"You can't keep food on the table if the bay is sick, either," David Watchman answered. "I'm finding some oil in your local water right now. Shouldn't be there; don't know where it comes from."

Ben felt a movement at his shoulder. It was his father, steering him away from the crowd.

"Well, what do you think, Dad?"

"I don't know, son. I don't like what that fella is saying. I don't much like any of it. Is that the scientist you were talking to?"

"Yes," Ben answered.

"What do you know about Little Bit Island? He been taking you out in his boat?"

"Just once, Dad. He took me and Matt. To get a crab for the race. We got home on time."

"He find oil in the water then?"

Ben remembered the black beads on the plankton net. "Yeah, Dad, just a little."

"Oil." Duke Warren hung his head, and then gestured at the marsh and the water alongside them. "Kills the birds. Kills the fish. Kills the marsh. What do you think? But don't you worry about it. You're going to be working in a fine office someday, just like Eddie. Now, let's go find your mother. She has a little surprise for you."

And what she had was a blue ribbon.

"Are you done making that stuff, Mom?" Ben asked, admiring her prize.

Mrs. Warren laughed. "No more crab soufflé, Ben. Corn season's coming, and watermelon." And she kissed him, right there in public. Ben forgave her, though, because she was so happy about winning and all.

5

In the middle of July, Matt went to visit his grandmother up in Baltimore for two weeks. It was very hot in Marsh Harbor then, and there weren't as many guests at the Warrens' bed-and-breakfast. The fishing was poor and it was too hot for sightseeing. Mrs. Jamison had gone off to a job picking crabs, and Ben had whole days off, but with nothing much to do. Although he begged his dad every day to take him out on the *Mary,* Duke Warren always cut Ben off with some little excuse: The weather report was uncertain, he had too far to go that day, or something.

One morning Ben bicycled out to the highway and started toward the next town. Sweat ran into his eyes, the cars smelled bad, and the greenhead flies began to bite. He stopped to rest at the new gas station. It had only been there about a year and was mainly used by tourists driving by on the highway. The place didn't even do any repairs, except oil changes and new tires and stuff like that. But it had a Coke machine and a bathroom. Since Ben didn't have any money, a man working there gave him a drink of water and let him sit awhile in the air conditioned office. Ben thought he was pretty nice. After a bit he felt better and started home. Then Matt's father came by in his pickup on his way back from the plant, and gave Ben a lift home. What a break!

That afternoon Ben decided to look up some other kids from school to see what they were up to. But as he walked past the dock, someone called out to him.

"Ahoy there." David Watchman waved from his outboard. "Where's your sidekick?"

"He had to go to his grandmother's."

"Tough luck. Want a ride? I'm headed up to the marsh."

Ben ran a few steps into the water, not bothering about his sneakers getting wet, and hopped over the side. There was even more equipment in the little boat today.

David pulled on the steering arm and the boat quickly bounced toward deeper water. It was cooler out there, with the added breeze from the boat, and there were fewer bugs. Ben cheered up a bit. He watched a flock of skimmers sweep over the water near them and then bank

64

up to the left, every wing tipping at the same moment.

"How do they know how to do that?" asked Ben.

"What?"

"Turn all at the same time like that."

"Well, I don't think anyone really knows. I imagine some fighter pilots would love to find out. Schools of fish do it, too."

"Do crabs?"

"No. Crabs are loners. You find a lot of them in the same place, but that's just because the food's good there. They don't really relate to each other, except for fighting and mating."

"Where do they mate? Out in the ocean?"

"No, as a matter of fact, they like to come up these little fingers of the bay where it's marshy. Crabs can only mate when they're molting; they can't do it with their shells on. And when they molt, they're easy for other fish to eat. So they come up here in the marsh and hide in the grasses. Then the eggs get washed out to sea, where they turn into little larvae-like things."

"Wow, I'd hate to be a little larva out in the ocean."

"Well, you've got that part right: Only about one in a million larvae makes it to be a crab."

"One in a *million*? Is that why there aren't too many crabs anymore?"

"No, the odds have always been like that. There were millions of crabs and every female lays over a million eggs. If only two of them lived, the number of crabs would remain steady."

"I see. So why doesn't it?"

"Well, the answer to that is compli-cated. There's more than one reason. One of them, I'm afraid, is that watermen like your Dad got so good at catching them that they can't reproduce fast enough anymore."

66

"My dad doesn't think that's the answer."

"Well, he's partly right, too. Another reason for the dwindling number of crabs is the loss of spawning ground. This grass we're coming to up here—" David cut the motor and let the boat drift. The grasses made soft swishing sounds against the bottom of the craft. "This is eelgrass, the stuff that grows underwater. But a lot of it's dying, so the crabs can't find as many good places to molt and lay their eggs."

"How come the grass is dying?"

"You ask good questions, Ben. And I'm partly working on trying to find the answers. That's why I look at places like this, too, where the eelgrass is starting to come back."

As they drifted through the eelgrass, David took several water samples. He covered each glass bottle with a little cork and set it carefully into a metal box. Then he picked a few leaves of the grass and examined them carefully. While he worked, some gulls swooped low past the boat, looking for bread or other free food. Disappointed, they made scolding sounds and flew off.

In the silence that followed, Ben asked, "How do you test the water?"

"Well, I'm going to do a number of things this time." David Watchman sat back, fingering the eelgrass. "First, we're going to check the temperature."

"They give the water temperature on the radio, you know," Ben said helpfully.

"That's true. But what they give is something that's approximately right, for swimmers or maybe for fishermen. I need to know the exact temperature, though, at different depths. I care about a difference of half a degree or so."

"Why?"

"Because then I'll know whether everything is in balance in this bit of water. At certain temperatures, certain salinities, and a certain Ph, you want a certain amount of dissolved oxygen and a certain number of phytoplankton."

Ben made a face. "Forget it. Are you going to measure all that?"

"Yup."

David handed Ben a line with a thermometer on one end. "Hold this right where I tell you," he commanded. "See that one foot mark? Okay, that holds the thermometer exactly one foot down. Good, now leave her there for half a minute." David looked at his watch. Ben couldn't believe half a minute could take so long. When he heard, "Okay, pull her up," he lifted the line. After David read the thermometer carefully, he took out a little notebook and wrote down the information. Then he handed the pole back to Ben. They had to make the same measurements at two and five and seven feet, and then the line hit the bottom.

"So," said Ben, "is the water healthy?"

David Watchman laughed. "We'll have

69

to analyze a lot of data before we know the answer to that."

Ben was not impressed. "My dad can tell when the water's healthy, just by looking at it. He knows by the color."

"I'm sure he does know a great deal," said David agreeably. "A person can get a feel from experience that takes science a long time to match. That doesn't mean, however, that science isn't more reliable in the long run."

Ben shook his head. It sounded contradictory to him.

Then David said, "I guess your dad doesn't like the new regulations too much."

Ben gave him a scornful look. "You got that part right."

"He's afraid his way of life is dying out."

Ben was thoughtful. Yes, he guessed that was it. "But it's not true, is it?" he asked. "I mean, the crabs aren't all going to just die, are they?"

"They're not an endangered species,"

said David. "But we do have some signs of trouble in the bay. The rockfish population is seriously down. You can't fish them at all now. The oysters are way down. And where you do have oyster beds, you have to keep checking them. Sometimes the oysters have filtered so much junk they're not fit to eat."

Ben knew that this was true. Several oyster beds and clamming spots nearby had been closed for the summer. Signs said CONTAMINATED AREAS. NO FISHING OR CLAMMING.

"But . . . " David hesitated. "Well, a lot depends on what happens from here on in. I think the bay can be saved. I even think you might be able to make a living on the water when you grow up. For that to happen, though, the government will have to step up its regulatory program, and the folks who live in the whole Chesapeake drainage area will have to learn to do some things differently."

"My dad says we'd be a whole lot better

off without the government," said Ben boldly. He looked at David and saw that smug look teachers sometimes had when they wanted you to find something for yourself. Suddenly Ben was furious. He wanted to go home. Swatting angrily at a fly, he snapped, "It's too hot out here."

They took one more measurement, then headed back in silence.

6

Matt got back from his grandmother's at last. He was full of talk about a big aquarium, so big you had to walk down a huge ramp past the tanks. He had seen flounder actually feeding on the bottom. And, he said, he had found out there was more to know about the bay than anyone could learn in a whole lifetime, even a scientist.

73

Ben asked his dad if they could go to the aquarium but, of course, they couldn't. A trip to Baltimore took time and cost money. And right then the crab harvest was good.

"I'm bringing home the bacon now, Mary," Duke Warren said happily in the evening. Once he even kissed his wife right at the supper table.

"Well," said Ben, still stewing over something exciting to do, "then you ought to at least take Matt and me out on the boat."

"Leave off bothering your father, Ben," said his mother.

"Wait a minute, Mary. With the crabs coming in like this, actually I could use some help. Can't afford to hire a culler right now. Won't hurt Ben. He's a good culler, but I don't know about Matt. Think he can stay out of trouble on a boat?"

"Yeah, he can, really, Dad. Matt knows how to sort crabs, almost as good as I do, even if his father isn't a waterman like you."

Duke smiled.

"Watch the weather," warned Ben's mother as she settled in to do her evening accounts. "And you better check with Matt's parents before you go taking him out."

Naturally, Matt's mother said yes. "Have a grand time," she told Matt as he left the house the night before the outing, to sleep over with Ben. "Stay out of Mr. Warren's way, Matthew, and do exactly as he says."

The boys set their alarm for four-thirty. It was the earliest Matt had ever gotten up.

"It'll be dark, you know," advised Ben.

"Great," said Matt.

But when the alarm buzzed that Saturday morning, four-thirty did not feel so terrific. Ben had been sound asleep, not even dreaming, not even awake listening for the sound of his father creaking around. He got up, shook himself and Matt, and pulled on his pants and shirt. The clothes felt cold.

When the boys arrived in the kitchen, Mrs. Warren was already there, wearing her long fuzzy bathrobe and with her hair all rumpled. Duke sat at the table eating a cold biscuit and tying his boots.

"Hey, there's my crew," he hailed Ben and Matt.

"Hey," answered Ben sleepily.

"Now you boys have some breakfast," said Mrs. Warren. "Your father goes off with a biscuit, but you two need something hot."

"We're late as it is, Mary."

Ben's mother ignored the comment. She spooned out two bowls of hot oatmeal, poured milk on top to cool it, and drizzled a bit of honey over that. Ben would have liked to eat just like his father, but the oatmeal smelled good. It tasted even better going down. Grown-ups got to drink coffee, Ben reasoned, to make them warm, so kids needed something of their own. He noticed that Matt was gulping down his oatmeal, too. "I thought I didn't like this stuff," Matt whispered.

As the three of them left for the dock, the darkness was lifting. You could see the outlines of buildings and the sky pale and huge. On the way, they passed other watermen.

"Morning, Duke. Got some helpers today, have you?"

"Morning, Ed. This here is my son Benjamin. He's my culler today. And his friend Matt."

"Good-looking boy, Duke."

Ben beamed. Something about the early morning seemed to make everyone more friendly. That was one reason, among the many, that he liked working the water.

At the skiff that was to take them to the *Mary*, Duke Warren got the plastic bushels of fish he had made ready the night before. He loaded them into the small boat and then the boys climbed in. The short ride was just as Ben remembered. The breeze was cool, and as the sun popped above the horizon, it sent a beam of red over the dark, smooth water. You could hear birds everywhere, the cry of a heron, the shrieks of gulls.

When they reached the *Mary,* Duke made the skiff fast to the mooring. Then he jumped into the big boat in one leap. Ben and Matt each needed a hand up. Looking back at the shore, Ben saw a dark line of trees with a halo of light over the crab shacks near the dock. He watched the fast-rising sun turn the trees and the water blue with golden sparkles, as if it were a giant painter.

Duke stood at the wheel and turned the key. Matt and Ben heard the engine rumble and felt the vibrations at their feet. They grinned at each other—it was really happening!

"Let go the mooring," Duke yelled. Ben leaned down and unhitched the rope from the big steel pin on the mooring buoy. Now Duke pushed the lever with the black knob, and the deck shivered as the engine slipped into gear. Then he pushed the red-knobbed throttle.

The *Mary* went fast, leaving a tumbling wake of white water behind. The boys rested easily against the side of the boat and watched things float by: white jellyfish and bits of weed, shadowy sea life, and once a dead fish. Passing Smith Island, they saw more boats heading out, some with big hydraulic dredgers on the back. Ben explained to Matt that his father used pots, not a dredge.

"Pots is a funny name for them," said Matt. "Why don't they call them traps? Wire crab traps, that's what they are."

"Well, they're called pots," Ben answered firmly.

After nearly half an hour at high speed, Duke suddenly cut the engine to neutral. The *Mary* slowed down until she floated up beside a little green-and-white-striped bobber, the marker for Duke's first pot. Green and white were Duke Warren's colors; every waterman's colors were different.

Now it was time to get dressed for work. Ben's father put on his oilskin apron and handed Ben and Matt each an old one. Then he passed out gloves, good sturdy rubber ones that would protect the boys' hands from the sharp claws of crabs or the stinging of sea nettles.

"Now then, Matt," said Duke, leaving the wheel. "Let me tell you about your job. You take this gaff hook here." He handed the boy a long wooden pole with a metal hook at one end. "You draw that hook under the line, like this here, and hook it onto the spool. That's the pot hauler." As he spoke, Duke caught the gaff hook under the line to the pot and hooked the line over a little wheel on the side of the boat. Matt nodded. It looked easy.

Then Duke pressed a lever and the

wheel turned, hauling the pot up from the bottom. Since the bay was only about six feet deep at this spot, it took less than a minute for the pot to break the surface of the water. Watching it rise, Ben laughed with excitement. Underneath the watery grass that clung to the wire, he could see a mass of crab bodies.

"Let me haul it in, Dad, can I?" Last year Ben had not been strong enough to lift the full pot over the side of the boat, heave it upside down, and pour the crabs onto the culling table. But now he was nearly eleven.

Duke Warren nodded. "Heave up, then."

Ben leaned over. This year his arms were just long enough to allow him to grasp the top of the pot. He pulled manfully, but it was harder than he expected to lift from a bending-over position. Inch by inch the pot emerged from the water. Ben saw the crabs scratching madly inside as they hit the air. Then he had the pot above the water, but suddenly his fingers gave way. As the pot splashed back, Ben's throat tightened with frustration.

"Hey, Ben," sang his father beside him, "that was a smart lift for a boy your age, better than I'd thought you'd do. One more year and we'll have you hauling pots with the best of them. Now you watch that table with Matt. I'm going to haul you some pots so fast you'll think it's raining crabs. Stand aside there. Ho!"

Ben did not have a moment to feel bad. As soon as the pot swooshed over the table, thirty crabs tumbled out helter-skelter, back side up and underside up, claws and legs tangled together. A few landed on the deck and slithered away, reminding Ben of the Fourth of July festival.

"Grab those sidesteppers, Matt," Duke Warren called out. "Now you go, Ben. Sooks on the left, jimmies on the right. You see any peelers, they go in that bucket of water. Hey, get along there.

We've got a right smart load of crabs."

While he was shouting orders, Ben's father moved the *Mary* gently alongside the next pot. Matt dumped the escaped crabs on the culling table and with the hook grabbed at the new line. A new pot came out of the water and was emptied on top of the first batch. Quickly, Duke grabbed a piece of herring bait, put it in the pot, and threw the pot back in the water. Then he edged the *Mary* on to the next.

Ben tried to move his hands faster and faster. It was hard working with the rubber gloves, and the crabs were always getting tangled up and biting at him. "Ow!" he said, eyeing the slice through his glove. Duke only laughed and kept the crabs coming. (There was no time to think, let alone to nurse small wounds.)

"Hey, throw that little fellow back, he's against the law."

Ben had forgotten all about little ones. A crab that measured less than five inches from point to point across its back was too little. He was afraid he had kept some already and cast a worried look at his father. But Duke Warren only shrugged. "No harm if there are others; just keep an eye out."

Ben thought that's what he'd already been doing, with his eyes moving as fast as his hands examining each underside. Soon he sorted the crabs automatically, without thinking sook or jimmy, left or right.

"Atta way to move 'em," said his father approvingly, and Ben's heart swelled. Although his feet hurt and his arms hurt, right then he did not care.

"Oh, look-ee here." Duke paused before he shook out the next pot. There were fewer crabs in this pot, and also a large fish caught by a fin. Ben glanced up and Matt came around from the side where he'd been hooking lines.

"Bluefish," Matt said with a smile. "My mom loves bluefish. She gets them from

Pat O'Brian. He gives them to her off his boat."

While he was talking, a brash gull flew in and snatched a crab right off the culling table. Matt swatted at it with the gaff hook, but the bird flew off shrieking.

"Well, someone else likes to eat, too," laughed Duke Warren. "Matt, this is for your mom tonight." He threw the fish to one side to keep, then poured the rest of the pot's contents on the table.

Another twenty minutes of work and Duke Warren was at the end of his first string of pots. He was pleased with his helpers and with the size of his catch. The culling table was a mess, with bits of crab legs and eelgrass and mud and shell and a slimy white jellyfish, called a sea nettle. Duke removed that carefully himself, because no one, he said, not even a grown-up, likes to be touched by a sea nettle.

Now there was a break while the *Mary* cruised to the next line of pots. The sun was high and felt hot on the boys' heads as they slowly wiped the table and threw the debris over the side. They had a snack of potato chips and root beer, and Duke drank some coffee from his thermos. He pointed out a huge sea clam dredger, headed out for the ocean, and a couple of little pleasure boats. There was a boy in one of the small boats. As it passed close by, Ben and Matt lounged professionally against the side of the boat, Matt holding the gaff hook carelessly over his shoulder. The boy stared, clearly impressed.

Then Duke pointed out a thin dark line of clouds back by Smith Island. "Got to keep our eyes on that. Could be trouble. Now the next line we're coming to here, this is deeper water and likely we'll be taking mostly jimmies. Got a good price for those this week, might be over twenty-five dollars a bushel today. We're making money, mates. You change off for a bit. Matthew, hand that hook to your shipmate. You know how to tell the jimmies? Look-a-here at this apron." Duke held a male crab upside down and showed Matt the marking. "And if they're small, you hold them up to this stick here." The stick was notched to show five inches exactly. "Otherwise we might get a little visit from the Coast Guard," said Duke with a wink. "Wouldn't do to start your career getting busted."

As they neared the first pot, however, Duke's high spirits vanished. Looking over the *Mary*'s sides, the boys could see why. Suddenly the water around them was thick and brown.

"What is that stuff, Dad?"

"Huh. Algae."

"I know what happened. It's because of fertilizer running off of farms and lawns. See, Dad, the fertilizer runs into the water, and it feeds the algae. So you get millions more algae than normal. Then the algae crowd each other and that uses up oxygen. So now, with all this algae dying right here, there's no oxygen left for the fish." Ben took a big breath. His father's sharp blue eyes were staring at him. "Or for crabs," Ben added.

"You been talking to that scientist?" Duke asked.

Ben hung his head.

His father continued, more sad than cross. "Well, I reckon he's got the right of it this time. I just wonder when he's going to figure out what to do about it."

Slowly and with no enthusiasm, Duke Warren hauled up the first pot by himself. He inspected the load carefully without pouring it over the culling table. Every crab was dead. He returned them to the water without comment.

Now they moved silently from pot to pot. The bustle and excitement were gone. The air in this part of the bay smelled of rot.

"How far did the algae bloom go, Dad?"

"No telling."

All fifty pots on the second line were

full of dead crabs. Duke Warren did not even bother to bait them, for he had no way of knowing when the water would be restored.

At last, he steered the *Mary* back up the bay, toward Smith Island again and another deep-water pot line. Within minutes, they were out of the dark water, and everyone's mood improved. While they cruised, Duke Warren passed out sandwiches. The wind had picked up, and as they ate they enjoyed the spray made by the bow slapping against the waves. Passing by a channel marker with a nest on top, they were just in time to see a heavy bird spread its great wings for a perfectly controlled landing.

"Osprey," said Duke Warren. "Used to be hardly any of those around."

"And now there's lots of them," added Matt. "I've seen them."

"Yes." Duke Warren shrugged and smiled. "For once those scientist fellows did something right." He seemed to be looking far off down the bay, toward the ocean. "It was DDT," he said at last. "The government made them stop using DDT. Now the birds are back."

"What's DDT, Dad?"

"What?" Mr. Warren stared at his son as if he had forgotten about him. "Well, DDT, that was before your time."

7

The next line of pots went along fine, except that Ben was tired. He took a turn with the gaff hook, but it was harder to manage than it looked. He couldn't figure out how you were supposed to know where the stupid line was. The water was too dark to see through. And then the line would fall off the hook while he was trying to load it onto the pot hauler, and he had to start over. As soon as he got finished with the line, he had to turn around and scoop scuttling crabs off the deck. His arms were tired, his back was tired, even his eyes were heavy. But his father kept the crabs coming in.

Matt was tired, too. "Phoo," he said out loud, as a particularly full pot was unloaded on the table.

Duke laughed when Matt stepped back and glared at the crabs. "In ten minutes, we'll be done with this line and heading home. Just hang in there."

That was good news. Ben was glad he had stuck it out the whole day, but he was glad it was almost over, too. He smiled at Matt, who shook his head and rolled his eyes, then dived after the crabs.

When the next pot was hauled in, Ben reached down for a fat jimmy that was headed toward the stern. Suddenly he felt a sharp sting across his face. In another second, the stinging became much worse, and he cried out, "Dad!"

"Ben!" Duke Warren's face registered alarm.

Ben's mind raced. What had happened? He felt his cheek and looked at his finger. No blood. Then he remembered. He had felt this same pain long ago when he was swimming in the bay and had brushed against a sea nettle with his leg. Now he watched his father pick the white, slimy thing off the pot where it had hung. It must have whipped him across the face as the pot flew by. Duke tossed the sea nettle into the ocean and bent over his son.

"Didn't get you in the eye, did it, Ben?" he asked.

"No, I don't think so. Just my cheek." He could hardly talk, the pain was so bad.

Duke Warren hurried to the bow and quickly returned with a little can.

"What's that?" asked Matt. "Paprika?"

"Meat tenderizer. Always keep some on board. It's the only thing I know for sea nettle stings. Here, Ben, take your hand away so I can put this on." Gently Duke patted the tenderizer onto Ben's already red and puffy cheek. Immediately, Ben felt better.

"Thanks, Dad," he said, wiggling his jaw. "Did you ever get stung by one of those things?"

"Lots of times. Didn't like it the first time, didn't like it after that. Some things in this universe, you've just got to wonder why God made 'em. I suppose they have a purpose. But for my money, you could have let the jellyfish population crash and kept up the rockfish."

Duke Warren patted Ben on the back, then rose from his knees. Suddenly he was thrown into the side of the boat. Ben and Matt were toppled on top of him.

"What the . . . ?" began Matt.

Before anyone could say another word, the *Mary* lurched violently in the opposite direction. Only Duke Warren got to his feet, and he moved fast. "It's the squall!" he yelled. But the sound was so scattered that the boys could scarcely hear the warning. Ben looked up. Matt's hair was standing almost straight on end, and behind him the sky was dark and boiling with clouds. He clutched at the side of the boat and pulled himself up.

Duke Warren was still yelling words that the boys could not hear, but they figured out their meaning. From somewhere he had pulled out two orange life preservers and he pushed them at the boys while grabbing at the wheel. The *Mary* was being tossed in every direction. Ben looked at his father's serious face, then he looked toward land. Yes, they were pretty far out, not where you're supposed to be when a squall hits.

A crack of lightning seemed to hit the water just a few feet from the *Mary*'s bow. Duke gestured wildly for the boys to get down. They crouched under the shelter of the culling table, pushing aside the heavy baskets of crabs to make room for themselves. The thunder came almost immediately, so loud that the boat seemed to vibrate with the sound. Matt shrugged his head into his shoulders and grabbed hold of Ben, who was glad for someone to hold on to. He squeezed Matt's arm and shut his eyes. His father had no life preserver. There were only two on the boat. A waterman who fell overboard often drowned because he couldn't swim in his heavy oilskin apron and rubber boots. Please, prayed Ben. Please let my father be all right.

The tossing and turning, the sickening roll of the boat continued. Ben heard a crash of glass. He opened his eyes. It was only his father's thermos, which must have knocked against the metal of the gaff hook. Duke Warren still looked very serious, very attentive, but perhaps just a trifle more confident.

Suddenly the water began to calm. Then what his father said about Chesapeake storms was true, Ben thought. They blow right up, then back right down.

"Look, Matt," said Ben. "We're okay now."

Matt stuck his head up. The dark squall line was past them. They could see a bank of dark clouds above, and a stripe of blue sky below. In between, where the sun shone from behind the clouds, was a golden band so bright they could hardly look at it. The water was still choppy, but it was nothing the *Mary* couldn't handle.

The boys crept out of cover and looked around. The rain had washed the deck and table clean. Droplets glistened everywhere as the sun came out stronger and stronger.

Duke Warren lit a cigar. "We're going home, boys," he said. "We've got a load of crabs here to sell, and I've got a crew that's done a real day's work."

Ben and Matt looked at one another.

They were soaking wet. Their clothes were dabbed with mud and smelled of fish. Their hair was wild and blown. Matt had a sore thumb from a crab bite, and one side of Ben's face was twice as fat as the other. They doubled over with laughter.

Duke got on his shortwave radio and shared news with several other watermen. The storm had hit lightly some places, badly others. Pat O'Brian was just touching in at the dock and promised he'd tell Mary Warren and Matt's mother that the boys were safe.

When they finally got into Marsh Harbor, it was late. Ben wanted to stay and help his father, to finish the whole day right, but Duke Warren insisted he get home for dinner. At the thought of food, Ben went willingly with Matt.

"You still going to be a waterman when you grow up?" asked Matt on the way back. He was swinging the dead bluefish in a plastic bag.

"Sure."

"Not me. I'd get too tired."

"You'd get used to it," said Ben. But he had to admit tonight he was tired, too. His legs hurt as he lifted them for the last steps into his house. And, once inside, he practically fell into a kitchen chair.

"Good grief," exclaimed his mother, examining him. "They about chopped you up to mincemeat out there." She gave him a cool bag of ice for his cheek, and then she took his shoes off as if he were a little boy. It was pleasant and warm in the kitchen and Ben appreciated his mother's babying. He drank the milk she brought him and winced a bit as she washed the little cuts all over his hands with a warm washcloth. Now the smell of hamburgers and carrots cooking made it hard to remember the odor of fish and muck. Ben closed his eyes. Behind them, he could still see pot after pot of crabs crashing onto the culling table.

"You get a good harvest today?" his

mother asked him, just as she asked his father.

Ben blinked. "Yeah," he said proudly. "We brought home the bacon today."

8

The next day at Sunday dinner Duke
Warren was full of praise for Matt and
Ben. "Yessir," he said, wiping his mouth
with his napkin, "those boys were a big
help and good company out there on the
water."

Ben said nothing, but felt proud all
over. His face was better today, though

his hands were full of scabs. He stirred his clam chowder and listened to the rain pattering against the family room windows.

"Eat up, Ben," said his mother, "before your food gets cold." She shot a warning glance at her husband.

Ben took a bite of clam and potato. "When I'm sixteen, I can leave school," he said boldly, "and help Dad with the winter tonging. He said it's bad to be out alone in the winter. Once Eddie's out of college, he won't ever help on the water."

But the day before had not swayed Duke Warren. "You're going to finish high school, you hear?" he said. "Your mother and I only want you to do your best, and the rest will follow. Don't be dreaming overmuch about spending your life on the bay. Anyway, the bay's changing. Look at all the new folks, hanging around town every day. They've got a new shop open, just to sell T-shirts. Have you seen that?" He turned to his wife.

"Yes, Duke, I've seen it. And the rooms at the new inn are not going begging, I've heard, even at sixty dollars a night. I'm thinking I'll raise our rate to forty."

"Mom," interrupted Barbara. "They sell neat bathing suits at that T-shirt shop, too."

Ben giggled and made his soup gurgle. He and Matt had stared at those suits—two-piece jobs, no bigger than handkerchiefs.

"Benjamin, mind your manners."

"There's talk about condos, too," Duke Warren went on. "Rafe says his aunt is selling her land, going to move to Florida. Looks like a developer has his eyes on it. People, people, always more people."

As if to prove his point, the front bell rang, the one that meant paying guests. Ben's mother hastily smoothed her hair and went to the door. Duke Warren frowned and sighed. Usually most of the guests had left by Sunday afternoon, and Ben and his family could enjoy an uninterrupted meal on Sunday evenings. But if someone rang then, you couldn't turn them away, not at forty dollars a night.

"Dad?" began Ben.

"Hush, son." His father was listening to the conversation in the front hall.

"My word, what have you been doing?" Mary Warren asked pleasantly. "Out on the water without your slicker, and on a Sunday, too?"

"You caught me this time." The man laughed. "I forgot to check the forecast this morning, and here I am, a drowned chicken."

"Have you eaten yet? The diners will be all closed now, except for the inn, and that's costly."

"Well, I imagine I can find a bit of something."

"No, you can't, take my word for it. Tell you what, I made a huge pot of clam chowder. Just take off your wet things, then come into the family room there, and I'll give you a bowl."

The visitor thanked her and then they heard Mary Warren bustling in the kitchen.

Ben panicked. He knew already by the voice that the man was David Watchman. Ben hoped that David would not greet him too heartily, for Duke Warren still did not know that his son had been out in David's boat a second time.

But David seemed to grasp the situation immediately. He ran his hand through his curly wet hair, winked at Ben, and then nodded and said soberly, "Ben, isn't it?"

Ben still wiggled uncomfortably. He hoped his mother didn't know what David had said to the watermen at the fair, or how Duke had warned Ben to stay away from him. Mr. Warren stood up to shake hands politely, but his face was sober.

Barbara tossed her hair. "Did you get caught out in the rain?" she asked sweetly.

"Yes, and my water samples are all pretty useless, because they're full of rain water. Make it look as if the bay is getting fresh, eh?"

"What do you aim to do with these water samples, once you get them right?" asked Duke.

Ben's mother came in and set down a bowl of hot chowder and a slice of home-made bread. David sampled the soup before answering Duke's question.

"I take them to a lab up at the University of Maryland. It's part of my graduate work. There's a lot of us doing this, taking water samples all over the bay."

"And can they tell us when the oysters are coming back?"

"No, they can't say for sure. A lot of biologists don't think the oysters are ever coming back, not in the numbers we used to have."

"Hmpf," snorted Duke. "There's been ups and downs before, before your time."

David nodded and went on eating. He

didn't seem to want to argue. Ben wondered whether that was because he was afraid of Duke, or just because he was so sure of himself.

"If these biologists know so much," Duke went on, "how come they can't do anything about it? What good is it to know there's not as many oysters? Every waterman on the Eastern Shore can tell you that. It doesn't take a team of experts to find it out." Duke watched David carefully.

"This is the finest chowder I believe I've ever had," the man said politely to Ben's mother. "You ought to serve it for breakfast."

"Why, thank you," she replied, "maybe I will."

"She won't be able to," Duke interrupted, "without clams from the bay. So what is the government aiming to do about it, if they do find something wrong with the water? You can name me all the chemicals in the ocean—"

"Duke," his wife warned gently.

"Depends what the problem is," said David Watchman calmly. "If there's a legal way to get someone to clean the contaminant up, that's what they'll do. But if there's no point source—"

"What's a point source?" asked Ben, forgetting that he was not supposed to interrupt when grown-ups were talking.

"It's government talk," said Duke.

David smiled. "Yes, I suppose it is. It just means, well, a point source is when some kind of pollution comes from one specific place, like a pipe going into the water." He leaned forward, eyes on Ben. "It's relatively simple. If you can turn off the pipe, you've solved your problem. Lots of times, there's just one group or company responsible, and you get after them. But non-point-source pollution, that's when the problem kind of seeps in from all over, or drains from many places far away. Like agricultural runoff."

"Like fertilizer?" asked Ben.

"Good for you. Like fertilizer. You know, the Chesapeake Bay starts out at the top of the Susquehanna River, way up in New York State. It picks up rivers in Pennsylvania and Maryland and Virginia, and it drains water from farmland and cities and suburban streets and just every-thing that's out there. So if you find a little bit of something in your water that you don't like, it can be pretty hard to say where it comes from. Sometimes it comes from everywhere."

There was a moment of silence. Barbara scooped a clam out of her chow-der and held it out on her spoon. "Yuck, you mean there's fertilizer in this thing?"

Everyone laughed, except for Duke Warren. "Never got sick eating out of the Chesapeake," he declared.

"That clam is almost certainly fine," agreed David. "It is amazing how nature has ways of cleaning itself, adapting, keeping our environment healthy." As if to back up his statement, he finished off his soup. Then he thanked them all for having him and retired to his own room.

* * *

The next morning Ben was actually eager to help with the breakfast service. Alas, David Watchman never appeared. As if that weren't bad enough, Ben's mother asked him to stay and help Barbara with the dishes. So it was after ten before he knocked on Matt's door.

"Wish we had a boat," said Matt. "Remember when Mr. Watchman said he found oil in the water? Don't you wish we could find where it came from?"

"Yeah," agreed Ben.

But the *Intrepid Voyager* was still sunk in the mud, right where they'd left her. So the two boys played the electronic basketball game that Matt had received the previous Christmas. They had already played it hundreds of times.

When a buzzing fly began to drive Ben crazy, he said, "Let's go find some clams, anyway. Remember when we used to get them up in the marsh at the end of Main Street? Where you cut your hand on that old oyster shell?"

"Yeah, I remember." Then Matt was more enthusiastic. "Hey, I know what. We can get a lot of crabs and clams and mussels and set up our own seafood stand. You know, for the tourists. With the money we earn, we can buy our own boat."

"Boats cost a lot, Matt," cautioned Ben.

"I know where you can get canoes for fifty dollars. Honest."

"It's too hot to go digging in the marsh. It's full of bugs."

"Naw, they won't be bad. It's been pretty dry. C'mon, Ben, let's go."

9

Careening up Main, Ben balanced Eddie's long-handled clam rake across the handlebars of his bike. He knew this was not a safe thing to do, but he certainly wasn't going to walk all the way to the marsh. It was about two miles away and he was right about one thing: It was hot.

The road turned to sand after he and

Matt passed the last turnaround by the high school. Their bicycle wheels spun in the sand, and it was hard for Ben to steer with the clamming rake over his handlebars. Finally, he got off and walked the last little bit. Matt didn't wait for him.

When he reached the high marsh near where a small freshwater stream came in, Ben spotted Matt's bike behind a wax myrtle bush. Throwing down his bike next to Matt's, he walked past the shrubs and into the marsh. Now it was covered with salt-meadow hay and the tiny purple blooms of marsh heather. The earth was dry because the ground here was only submerged in the big spring tides. Ben looked about. He could see straight out over the low marsh to the bay, but he did not see Matt.

Swatting a greenhead fly that bit him on the arm, Ben followed the stream. Where the stream and low marsh met, cordgrass grew long and thick and green. When the tide was coming in, the water would seem to flow upstream, sending saltwater way on up the creek. But now it was flowing down toward the bay and toward the ocean. At the low marsh, the ground was damp, and hundreds of fiddler crabs scurried toward their holes as Ben passed by.

"Hey, Matt!"

"Quit yelling, will you?" Matt's voice was right at hand. Although the cordgrass looked like a level prairie of green stems where nothing could hide, actually a person bending down could easily disappear from sight. Indeed, Matt's curly head appeared above the grass, as if by magic. "Look what I found," he said, grinning. Following the bend in the creek, he emerged from the grass with a small flat-bottom fiberglass boat in tow. A frayed rope was tied to its bow.

"Oh, man, terrific!" exclaimed Ben. "Where was it?"

"Just floating, right there where I was standing. Wasn't tied up or anything.

Must have torn loose from somewhere—look at the end of this old rope. Maybe got loose in that squall we were in."

"Hey, man, we can pole it with the clamming rake!"

Gleefully, the boys looked out over the acres of cordgrass that spread out between them and the bay. Before, getting around the marsh had always been a matter of sinking in the mud or balancing on little tufts of cordgrass roots. They never got far, and they had to stay near the high end of the marsh. But now they could follow the creek in the boat and end up in deeper water. "Maybe we can find oysters," said Ben.

The boys got into their new boat, and Ben took the first turn with poling. Standing, he pushed the end of the rake into the mud and then threw his weight forward. The boat slid silently through the water. As Ben withdrew the rake and started on another pull, the ooze gave a little sucking noise. In minutes, their starting place was out of sight.

Another greenhead bit Matt, who slapped vigorously and got him. In the midafternoon hush that covered the marsh, the sound was startling. While he poled, Ben stared dreamily into the water. Forgetting clams or oysters, he watched instead the reflections of the puffy white clouds overhead. The gut had many twists and turns, and Matt had to pull at the cordgrass along the sides of their narrow passageway to help the boat slip through. Gradually the channel widened.

The boys stopped to admire a pure white egret standing on one long black leg. Paying no attention to the oncoming boat, the bird only eyed the water. Its long neck was poised and still and then, suddenly, its bill shot down into the muck and up again. The boys could see the legs of a small crab struggling from the tip of the bird's bill. In another moment, the egret swallowed and the crab was gone.

116

Matt and Ben began to laugh out loud.

The noise drew the bird's attention. It stared at the boys, then slowly and quite unafraid, it spread an enormous pair of wings and flew off over the marsh.

"That was neat," said Ben. His voice was still low, he realized, for no reason.

"Wish we could catch crabs like that," said Matt.

"Yeah." Ben leaned against his pole, resting. He grasped a piece of cordgrass as it slid beside the boat and ran his finger along a smooth grassy leaf, rubbing off the layer of salt. Licking his finger, Ben looked down in the water. Among the stems of cordgrass, he saw some baby fish. "What are those things?" he asked Matt. "Baby menhaden?"

"Baby bluefish?"

"I bet there's eels hiding in there." Just then Ben saw a shape that he knew for sure, something like a clump of dark rocks growing off the bottom of the creek. Oysters! He was sure his mother would like them even better than crabs, because this was crabbing season.

"Nobody takes oysters in summer," Matt cautioned. "I think it's against the law."

"Aw, only a few," said Ben. "Besides, they're big ones. I wouldn't take them if they were small. There's too many dang government regulations around here, anyway." He thought his father would be proud to hear him say that.

"Don't cut yourself."

Ben used the rake to knock the oysters off their perch. It was hard, sweaty work, but he got half a dozen. When he was done, he noticed that the sweat seemed to beckon the greenheads, so he handed the pole off to Matt. "Here, get us out of here."

They glided into more open water now, and Ben leaned over the side of the boat to create a shadow so he could see the bottom. There were old scallop shells in this part of the marsh, which meant there might be live scallops around. Ben wished they had brought a net.

Distracted by another shadow, he looked up to see an osprey flying over them, on its way out to the bay. Maybe it was headed for a nest on one of the channel markers. The bird flew straight across the sun, which was getting noticeably low.

"Wonder what time it is?" said Ben. "Looks late. Boy, am I gonna catch it. Which way is back? Where'd we come in?"

The boys looked toward land. Now they were at the bay edge of the marsh, and the tide was low. A dozen little guts seemed to be flowing toward them. Which one had they come down?

"Tide is low," said Ben. "Even if we return the right way, we won't be able to get back up to the creek."

"We can always walk."

"Yeah, in the mud." Ben sighed, slapping at another fly.

There was nothing to do but to choose

a gut and head up. Although they might come out a mile from where they had left their bikes, they couldn't be completely lost—as long as the town was on one side and the bay on the other. Ben took another turn poling, but it was harder going up, and the boat had to slide over the mucky bottom more often. Then the water got deeper, and for a bit, poling was easier. Still, Ben would have wished to be home now.

"Holy smokes," he heard Matt say, in a kind of awe.

Ben looked up. Suddenly, in a large patch all around them, the marsh was dead. The cordgrass was brown and matted and turning to slime, and the air was heavy with a sickening smell. There were little oily rainbows on top of the water, and where a tump of cordgrass stood high, a dead fish lay on it. The silence here was different. It made you aware that a good marsh was full of tiny sounds, of birds and insects and windblown grass.

In this place only the flies seemed to survive.

"What happened? Where are we?"

"I don't know," answered Ben. "But we've definitely got to tell David Watchman about it. How can we remember where this place is?"

"There's a tree over there," Matt pointed out.

"Must mean solid land." Ben made for the tree, but their boat wouldn't budge. He looked into the thick water and saw that they were lodged against the edge of a metal barrel. "Look, Matt. Must be something in this barrel. I think we found some oil, all right."

"Yeah, but how are we gonna get out of here?"

The boys studied the situation. The boat wouldn't move, and they soon saw why. A half a dozen barrels blocked their way to the tree. The idea of getting out and walking in the stinking mess was gross. Then Ben saw three greenheads on his arm at once and felt a mosquito on his face.

"All right," he said to Matt. "We've got no choice but to leave the oysters, leave the clamming rake, and walk. Don't step on the barrels; they'll turn and you'll fall in. Try to keep your hands out of the water."

"It's probably poisonous," said Matt grimly.

"You bet," said Ben. "Don't drink any."

From opposite sides of the boat, the boys stepped gingerly into the slime. The tree was about ten yards away, or maybe twenty-five steps, by Ben's calculation. He prayed the water wouldn't get any deeper. Next to the boat, it came halfway up his shin. It felt warm, too, and left a ring of dark oil on his jeans. He wondered if oil would ever wash off. Boy, was he going to catch it.

Never had twenty-five steps seemed so long. Once both boys fell, but, tumbling onto each other, they each managed to hold the other guy up. Closer to the tree, the water became shallower and the ground firmer. But then there was junk to step over: some old batteries, a clutch plate, some tires. Steadying himself on a barrel, Ben noticed it felt heavy and full. So there might be even more of this gunk, he thought, ready to seep out into the marsh. He imagined the seep, spreading little by little, day by day, eating another acre and another acre of marsh, then consuming the bay, little by little. The idea of it almost made him sick. Maybe his father was right. Maybe the bay was doomed. Because what could be done, what could even David Watchman do about dead marshes like this? The smell of old oil filled Ben's chest, and he thought he might throw up.

When he finally reached the tree, he was covered with bites and oil. Matt was a sight, too.

"Wow, are we going to catch it," Ben said.

"Thanks," said Matt morosely. "How do we get home, anyway, so we can start catching it?"

They looked about for signs of something familiar. The tree was a large oak, and it was indeed on dry ground. Beneath it were many tire tracks, so many they created a shadow of a road. There were a few beer cans around, too.

The boys followed the tire tracks over a field full of weeds and onto a little road. It was paved, but narrow, like a driveway, and it was half covered with blown sand. Which way to turn?

"We must have floated north, up past where Main ends," Ben reasoned, looking at the sinking sun. "So I think we should turn right."

They did, and in less than a quarter of a mile, they were back on Main, just beyond where they'd dumped their bikes. Ben figured it was past dinnertime. He wasn't hungry, but he wondered if that oily smell was what was killing his appetite. He hoped the stench would partly blow off as they rode home.

At the corner by the Dari Dreme, Matt and Ben called quick good-byes. A couple of tourists on the sidewalk stared at them and wrinkled their noses. Oh boy, thought Ben once more, am I going to catch it this time.

10

On the back porch steps, Ben noticed that his sneakers were leaving black traces. He took them off and tossed them back into the yard. Inside the house, he removed his pants. They were black, too, from the knees down. Barbara saw him first.

"Boy, are you gonna catch it," she sang,

126

then burst out laughing. "Hey, Mom, he's in his underpants!"

Mary Warren rushed to the door. "Ben, where . . ." Her anger died as she looked at him. "Benjamin, what have you done to your pants?"

"I'm sorry, Mom. I really am. They got oil on them. At least, I think it's oil."

"And all over your face, and in your hair . . ." She touched him just a little, astonished. Ben felt his hair, then looked at his hand. Black.

"See, Mom," he began. "Me and Matt went up to the marsh. We were gonna get some clams and stuff to sell. And then we found this dead place. . . ."

"Benjamin," Duke Warren's voice thundered, and Ben was silent. "Come in here."

Ben looked at his mother, but she only took his pants and nodded toward the family room. Ben winced and cautiously stepped into the room.

His father was standing up. "You are

exactly one and a half hours late." He held out his watch so Ben could see it was true. "Here your mother's been calling Matt's mother, both of them—all of us—worried sick. You're covered with filth, too. I don't want to hear your excuses. If you weren't ten I'd lay you across my knee."

Ben felt tears coming to his eyes. It wasn't fair. It wasn't his fault. And his father wouldn't even listen to him.

"You'll go to bed without your supper," his father went on. "And I don't want you to leave the house for a week. You hear me?"

"I know, Dad, but you see—"

"I don't want to hear about it."

Ben turned his head away, and then anger got the better of him. "Well, *you* come in late, and *you* get Mom all worried, and we have to listen to *you!*" he roared. He couldn't help it; the words just fell out of him. He waited. He shouldn't have talked back.

But Duke Warren barely moved. He

just said, quietly and evenly, "Go up to your room right now."

And Ben went.

For a while he cried silently into his pillow. He was very hungry. His shoulder ached from poling; indeed, he seemed to ache all over. After a while, exhausted, he fell asleep.

He awoke suddenly from a bad dream. In the dream, he saw the egret flying, flying, dipping, coming down to land. Then it raised itself up, but it could not move. He felt the bird, desperate to flap its wings. Then he saw that they were trapped in an oozy bed of oil. The black gunk was rising higher and higher over the white bird, and its bill was moving as if it were trying to say something. . . . Ben woke up. He looked at the clock. Just after ten. His mother and father would be asleep by now. And Barbara, too. But David Watchman? Was he here tonight? Was he awake? Which room?

Quietly, Ben put on a clean pair of

pants and crept down the back stairs to the kitchen. He got an apple and a piece of bread, and then tiptoed to his mom's desk in the front hall. A little night light was burning there. He opened the guest book. Yup, the man was here. David Watchman, room four.

Ben ran back upstairs. Like a mouse he knocked on the door to room four. David Watchman opened it. Ben put a finger to his lips.

David raised his eyebrows and whispered, "I thought I heard you earlier. Your parents were in a snit this evening."

"I know. But listen, I have to tell you about something." David motioned Ben inside his room, and Ben found a seat on the edge of the bed.

David listened attentively while Ben told the whole story between bites of bread and apple. "I knew it!" the young man said excitedly. "That oil had to have a point source. Now can you tell me exactly where this place is?"

"Better than that, I can show you," Ben said. Then he remembered that he was grounded. "No, I'll just tell you . . . No, I better show you." He decided not to mention to David that he wasn't supposed to leave the house. "Tomorrow?"

"Right. You on breakfast duty in the morning?"

"Yes, as usual." Ben thought fast. His mother would probably have him making extra beds tomorrow. But when he was done, he could say he was going to his room, and then he could sneak out. He remembered that his mother had an appointment to talk to the contractor about a new wing tomorrow. "Tell you what," he finally said, "meet me in the high school parking lot, right after lunch, maybe twelve-thirty."

"Why not here?"

"Never mind; it's best to meet you there. I'll have my bike, but we can walk to the marsh from the high school."

The next day, everything worked as

Ben had planned. After devouring a huge breakfast, he helped his mother for a long time. Although she was still cross, she was eager to listen to his side of the previous day's events, like where the oil had come from. After he told her, she just shook her head. "The messes some people make."

"Do you think you could tell Dad? Do you think he could do something about it?"

Sadly, Mary Warren shook her head again. "No one can do anything about it. Folks just don't want to take care of the water, that's the way it is."

*　　*　　*

At noon, Ben's mother left to keep her appointment. He had a quick sandwich and then flew up Main on his bike. He would have liked to bring Matt along, but he didn't want to risk facing Matt's mother. And besides there was no time to get him.

David was waiting at the school, sitting on the back steps. Ben left his bike behind a bush and led the way up the road, to where the faint tracks led off across the field. In the bright sunlight, the big oak tree was easy to spot. As they neared it, Ben and David saw what looked like new tire tracks. Could whoever it was have brought a fresh load of barrels to dump?

Passing the tree at the edge of the marsh, David Watchman cried out, "Oh, it's even worse than I imagined. I expected to find one or two barrels, figuring you might have exaggerated. But look at this, half an acre at least. And everything dead." He knelt down and touched a little bit of the oily muck, fingering and then sniffing it. "It's oil, all right. This isn't one person dumping. This is an operation."

"Isn't there a law against dumping oil?" asked Ben.

"You bet there is. But the first question is, Who's doing it? Let's see if there's any identification on these barrels." He walked into the muck and began turning over a floating drum and examining it carefully. "Whoever did this didn't want to get caught," he said. "They haven't left any traces, no letters, numbers, or any ID. Too bad we can't stake it out."

"Why can't we?" asked Ben.

"Well, the local police just don't have the resources, and I doubt if I can get the state police interested."

"But what about you and me? We could watch here all night, many nights, until they come. Then we can catch them."

David said no, seriously, firmly. "You would have to watch every night for a month. And besides, people who get caught doing illegal things are usually very dangerous. The guys driving the truck, they know what they're doing is illegal, or they wouldn't be sneaking around like this. They may be sent in by some big company, or they might be in business to get rid of waste, and they just take this shortcut instead of finding a responsible place to dump. Responsible places tend to cost a lot more money."

Ben looked downcast.

"I know how you feel," David went on. "I'd like to get these guys, too. But they might even have a gun, you can't tell. Promise me, now, you'll stay away from this place. I'll file a report, and the state will take steps to clean the place up."

But that could take months, Ben thought. And in the meantime, maybe more barrels would come, and the oil would keep oozing. And the bay would keep dying, and his father would keep getting discouraged. Finally, there would be no future as a waterman for Ben Warren.

Wasn't it time for someone to really do something?

When David and Ben returned to the Warrens', David went to room four to pack his things—he would be gone for at least a week—and Ben sneaked up the back stairs, hoping his absence hadn't been discovered. Before he said good-bye, David gave Ben a piece of paper with a phone number written on it. "You can always reach me here early in the morning, and sometimes in the evening. If you find anything else, call me right away. But Ben, don't do anything dangerous."

Ben nodded, tucking the slip of paper carefully into the back pocket of his jeans.

11

When the house was still that night and
only the little light at the front desk was
on, Ben descended the front stairs and
left by the front door, which was farthest
from his parents' bedroom. Outside, the
street was dark. Once his eyes adjusted,
however, Ben realized that there was
some light, and that, in fact, the moon was

about to rise over the water. Perfect. Who wouldn't choose, he thought, the light of the full moon if you wanted to drive into the marsh in the dark. And a full moon meant a big tide. At high tide, Ben reasoned, the dumpers would have the best chance of driving close to the marsh without sinking too much.

A light was still on in Matt's room. Ben threw a pebble against the window, and after a bit Matt stuck his head out.

"Hey, Ben." Softly.

"Hey, Matt. Come down."

"I need to put some clothes on."

As soon as Matt got outside, the two boys hid around the corner of the house. Ben told his friend about the plan. They would have to wait in the marsh. They would also have to hurry, because the dumpers would be moving quickly, too. And, remembering David Watchman's warning, no heroics, no jumping out and yelling at anybody.

"Why don't we just tell the police?"

asked Matt. "We go right by the station anyway."

"Because," said Ben. "Because David says they can't do much about it. And, besides, they wouldn't listen to kids."

Matt agreed. He only went back inside for supplies. Paper and pencil to write down the license number. Snacks. Jackets, in case it got cold. He got everything but, for snacks, he could only find a couple of old oranges. Now they were ready to set out.

It was eerie bicycling in the dark. The Dari Dreme was closed, and most of the lights in the houses were out. In town, Main had street lamps, but the circles of light did not meet. So they rode through a pattern: darkness, light, darkness, light. Ben did not like riding into the dark, where he couldn't see, but he didn't like being in the light, either, where someone might see them and wonder what they were up to. Maybe they shouldn't be doing this after all, he thought. But he didn't share his doubts with Matt.

A car passed, but it didn't stop.

As soon as they got beyond the street lamps, they could see better without that on-off pattern of light. The moon was well up now and, approaching the marsh area, Ben and Matt could see it reflected over the water. As they pedaled along the narrow road, their bike tires made hissing noises in the sand. Finally, they reached the field.

In the moonlight, it was hard to detect the faint track marks. Hiding their bikes in the shadows at the side of the road, Matt and Ben headed toward the big oak tree, which loomed dark against the lighter sky. With that as a landmark, how could they get lost?

Matt tripped once in a hole in the ground. But he was okay. And once they heard an owl that made them jump.

At last they reached the tree. It seemed more friendly than the field, which was full of little night rustlings. Under its protective shelter, they ate their oranges.

"You ever been up all night, Ben?"

"Nope. You?"

"Nope."

Once the oranges were all gone, there was nothing to do but sit, wait, and listen. They could smell the oil when the breeze blew their way.

"What'll happen to you if your parents catch you?" asked Ben.

"Why would they catch me? They're asleep."

"Yeah, but I mean, if they did."

"Well, I'm already grounded. I guess they could take my bicycle. Or make me write the whole multiplication table, like Miss Thompson did."

Ben thought that, for him, it would be worse than that. He leaned against the tree and thought about his room, and his bed, and the bed where Eddie used to sleep, and his rock collection, and the certificate he got last year for reading enough books to get a free pizza at Pizza

Hut, only there wasn't any Pizza Hut around so he still had it. His rear end was getting damp. He wished he could be back in his room now.

The two of them must have fallen asleep because the next thing Ben knew there was a loud sound of shifting gears, almost in his ear, and headlights were cutting two sharp bands of brightness over the marsh. A truck was lumbering toward the tree.

Ben grabbed at Matt, who seemed groggy, too, and hissed, "Behind the tree." Hastily they crawled into the shadows. Ben's heart was beating so loud he could hear it. His hands shook. It was really them!

The driver must not have seen the two spies. When the truck turned around, backing up toward the marsh, Ben got a good look: green Ford pickup, license number PR 399. He didn't know where Matt had put the paper but he was determined to remember the number. He

repeated it under his breath. PR 399.
PR 399.

Two men got out of the truck, leaving
the doors open. Hurrying, they went
around to the back. Neither spoke, but
Ben could hear them grunting. A barrel
scraped along the bed of the truck. Then
there was a splash.

"Let's split," said a voice, and both men
ran back and hopped into the cab.

Ben saw the driver as he got back in.
He knew that man. Where had he seen
him before? Somewhere, somewhere.
He was a local man, Ben was sure of
that. Not a waterman—he was sure of
that, too.

The truck backed and turned, almost
hitting the oak tree behind which the
boys were crouched. Then the engine
revved, and the pickup was gone, the
headlights dimming across the field. Ben
and Matt stood up and watched it retreat.
As the truck neared the road, the headlights went out altogether.

"They're not taking any chances of being seen," Ben observed.

"But they *have* been seen!" crowed Matt. "Wow, we did it!"

"We're not done yet," said Ben. "Let's get out of here."

The boys dashed back across the field and found their bikes. As they whizzed down Main, Ben noticed that dawn was just breaking. They must have been out all night. Matt would probably get into his house all right, but he would have to watch out for his father.

Sure enough, the light was on in the Warren kitchen, and from under the open window Ben could smell coffee. He waited. He did not hear his mother's voice. He prayed this would be one of the mornings she slept through until six. Soon the front door opened, and the sound of his father's footsteps faded in the direction of the dock.

Quick as a cat, Ben whisked himself inside, up the stairs, and into his room.

Silently, he closed the door and, throwing his clothes on the floor, fell into bed. "PR 399," he murmured. And was fast asleep.

"Beeeeeen-jy! Seven-thirty." It was Barbara's voice. He knew he was home, safe. And he remembered: PR 399.

Suddenly full of energy, Ben threw back his blanket, climbed out of bed, and snatched up his jeans. There was David's number, still in his back pocket. It had gotten a little damp from the night before, but Ben could still read it. He put on the pants and dashed into the upstairs hall. From the top of the steps, he could hear his mother and Barbara in the kitchen. He picked up the phone and dialed.

12

"Hello?"

"David? Hey, it's me, Ben."

"Ben. What's happening?"

"We got it, David. We caught them. Me and Matt, we went up there last night and this truck came, it's a green Ford pickup—"

"Oh no, oh no, are you all right?"

"Sure, we're all right." Ben let out a breath, realizing it was true. They were all right. And now David would help them, would know what to do next. "We got their license number. Have you got a pencil?"

There was a short pause. "I don't believe it," said David's voice. "I don't believe you actually did it. All right, shoot. What's the number?"

"PR 399."

"Maryland?"

"Right," Ben answered, "Maryland."

"Maryland PR 399. All right, kid. You hold on tight there, and don't say a word. I don't want anyone skipping out of town. And I don't want you kids involved in this any more than necessary. You're going to see some action now. Was it someone local? Could you tell?"

"One of them is, anyway. I've seen him around, but I can't remember where."

"Terrific. We'll get them now, Ben. And one day old man egret is going to fly into that dead marsh, white as the driven snow." David Watchman began to chuckle. "Bye."

"Bye."

Ben put down the phone, full of happiness. That morning he didn't mind helping with breakfast, he didn't mind cleaning a room. He even offered to vacuum the front hall.

"Good heavens," said his mother. "I guess a few days around the house has made you a real helper. I'll talk to your father tonight about letting you out again."

But by nightfall, everything had changed. There was never any talk about letting Ben out again, because no one remembered that he'd been grounded, until nearly a year later. Then they all laughed about it, even Duke.

The first time Ben knew of something strange happening was that afternoon. He was in his room reading an old bird book that usually sat undisturbed in the hall bookcase. His mother came in, a funny look on her face.

"Benjamin, the police have called."

He tried for a split second to look upset, but it was no use. He grinned.

"They wanted me to know that you are not in any trouble, and that you have done a fine thing. They want you to come down to the station to tell them exactly what you saw. I guess you know what this is about."

"Sure, it's about the marsh. Will Matt be there too?"

"Matt, too."

"And you're not mad?"

"Well, I can hardly make up my mind. I'm surprised, even shocked, is what I am. I've never dealt with the police like this before, but they seemed so nice. The man kept saying, 'It's a fine thing your boy has done.' I think they have spoken to your father already. He was in early with a big catch, and he heard talk about it, down at the dock."

"Do we go right now?"

"Yes, now. The officer said your father is at the station. I'll leave Barbara to take care of things here."

She made him wash his face and put on a clean shirt, and then they walked the short distance to the station. A lot of people were there—Matt and his mother, Duke Warren, and three policemen, which was an enormous number for Marsh Harbor.

The plain little room with the flag and the desk was crowded. Duke Warren smiled at Ben, but before they could speak, one of the policemen put his hand gently on Ben's elbow.

"Come along, son," he said. Ben was frightened as he looked up and saw the insignia of the state police on the officer's shoulder. But the trooper smiled. "Your parents are mighty proud of you," he added, leading Ben through a door behind the desk.

Ben had never seen this part of the police station. It was a tiny room, with a chair and a little table holding a pad and pen and a tape recorder. When the tall trooper sat down, he made the table and chair seem too small. The handcuffs hanging from his belt clanked against the chair. Ben knew that he was not in trouble, but still he could feel his heart beating fast.

"Now," said the trooper, "I am going to turn on this tape recorder, and I want you to tell me exactly what happened, from the time you and your friend Matthew went off to look for clams."

So Ben took a deep breath and began to tell. He explained how he and Matt found the oil barrels and the dead place, and how he had told David Watchman, and why he decided to go back at night, even if it might be dangerous. The officer wanted to know exactly where the place was and what time the truck came. Of course, Ben didn't know the time exactly, but he described how his father was just going out when he got home. The man nodded as Ben talked.

"And the license number on the truck?"

"PR 399. Maryland, PR 399."

Then the trooper turned off the recorder and thanked Ben. He said that his account agreed perfectly with Matthew's. That was good. The bad part was that Ben had been doing dangerous things and not obeying his parents, and the trooper gave him a little lecture about that. Ben listened politely. Finally, the man congratulated Ben for reporting a criminal activity that endangered the whole community. Ben found it all a little confusing.

"Did you get the guys who did it?" he asked at last.

"Sure. The truck was from that new gas station out on the highway. They were taking in waste materials from a couple of dozen stations around the county. Quite a racket!"

Suddenly Ben remembered where he

had seen the man: at the gas station, that hot day when he rode his bike. And the man had been nice and had given him a drink of water.

"What will they do to them?" Ben asked.

"They may go to trial. It will be up to the judge. Your evidence here will be a big help. Probably the state will fine them and make them clean up the site," answered the trooper. "But that might not be the end of it. The mayor of Marsh Harbor has already called a special town meeting to discuss a new ordinance. Maybe you boys would be interested in going to that meeting to see what you started."

Ben was silent. He never thought what he and Matt did would be such a big deal.

When he finally returned to the front of the police station, Matt and his mother were gone. Duke Warren put an arm around his son's shoulder as they went outside.

"So, rascal," he said, "been sneaking out at night to look after the bay, have you?"

Ben looked up to see whether his father was kidding or not. "You're not angry, are you, Dad?"

"No, Ben," Duke answered seriously, "on balance, and considering everything, I'm proud. I've been on the phone with your scientist friend. I was satisfied he didn't put you up to this. The man has a head on his shoulders, I must say. And he certainly likes *you.*"

"You know, Ben," his mother said thoughtfully, "you ought to come with us to the town meeting to hear what everyone else thinks about this mess. The ordinance they'll be talking about will be printed in the paper tomorrow. When I've studied it over, I'll explain it to you."

"And to me, too," put in Duke, with a smile at his wife.

* * *

That Saturday night, the Methodist church was packed. It looked like all the town's grown-ups had come to the meeting—even some that Ben didn't recognize—but not so many children. In fact, he and Matt were almost the only ones. They sat together, right up near the front, with Ben's family on his side and Matt's family on his. Even Eddie showed up. He said the story about the oil dump made the papers in Salisbury and he had to come see his celebrity brother. Besides, he was tired of summer school and overdue for a trip home.

But Ben could not think about Eddie now. He was nervous. At home, his father kept saying they ought to just outlaw new people on the bay altogether: no new business, no new houses, period. But his mom loudly disagreed. She wanted the new wing on her bed-and-breakfast, and, she explained, the new ordinance almost would outlaw new people. It would be a rule that for the next ten years, Marsh Harbor could not enlarge its sewer capacity.

"Is that like the drain pipes for all the houses?"

"Right, Ben. And since the sewers are already about full, this ordinance would mean that we couldn't build many more bathrooms in Marsh Harbor."

"And gas stations always have bathrooms, right, Mom?"

"You bet, Ben. And so do restaurants, motels, marinas—"

"And wings on guesthouses," interrupted Duke. "You see, Ben, it would be hard on your mother, but I say it would be good for Marsh Harbor. We've done enough for people visiting this town. They bring in too much pollution."

Ben hated it when his parents disagreed. And, anyway, he was afraid that he might see that man from the gas station at the meeting. He had this awful nightmare that the man would stand up in the big room and say, "I gave this boy a drink of water when he was hot, and look at the thanks I get!"

Finally the mayor stood up and began the meeting. Ben found it hard to concentrate on what the man was saying—he was like a boring teacher. But it was clear the purpose of the meeting was to discuss the new ordinance. Ben tuned in and out as the mayor explained that the town's sewage system was already strained, and that it would take a major overhaul to add capacity without leaching into the surrounding marshes.

Ben remembered all the things his parents had said. His mother had argued that Marsh Harbor should make sure the sewage system wasn't overworked. "You have to plan for what might happen in a storm," she'd said, "with all that extra rainwater." But Duke Warren had countered that it was good to be on the old small system because that way you didn't get all the traffic, dirty air, and trash. Ben couldn't decide what he thought.

Now it was time for discussion. One of Ben's neighbors stood up and said he wanted to build a garage. The mayor assured him that he still could do so under this new law.

Then another Marsh Harbor man spoke up. He said that he was in favor of any plan to limit growth. "I'm sick of the way Marsh Harbor is changing," he shouted. "I can't even go to the hardware store without waiting in line with a lot of tourists. Traffic is terrible. You can't park in town any more. Pretty soon taxes are going to go up. We locals will be paying for services for a lot of summer people. And it's not worth it."

Lots of people clapped. Then someone else got up and said just the opposite. "If you want to talk money, growth is the way of the future. Everyone knows the fishing industry is dying. But tourists mean jobs. Why, the new gas station itself, which was recently fined, thanks to the efforts of some local boys, provided steady jobs for at least three Marsh Harbor natives. It was a necessity for people traveling through by car. And people in cars are a source of business. Look at the T-shirt store, the diners, the new Marsh Harbor Inn, the guesthouses." There were more murmurs all around as the speaker sat down. Mary Warren nodded approvingly.

A well-dressed woman stood up, a stranger to Ben. She said that as for traffic, that didn't have to be a problem. You could widen the roads, and there was an excellent spot for a parking lot if you knocked down the old Dari Dreme. She said more about money and taxes that Ben didn't understand at all.

When Matt's mother volunteered to speak, Ben put his head down low so no one would notice him. She said she didn't want Marsh Harbor turned into a lot of streets and parking lots, and that was that. Her remarks were greeted with both boos and cheers.

Matt's father said they had an example directly before them, of what happened when you allowed growth. Here was the new gas station polluting the marsh, with no regard for the environment the townspeople had always respected. He for one was proud of his son for his role in catching the culprits. There was some polite applause then for the boys. Ben ducked further in his seat.

His head whirled. There were such good reasons for Marsh Harbor to grow, and such good reasons for it to stay small. More people talked, but he didn't pay any attention. He was thinking. Looking around the room, he spied David Watchman. Their eyes met and then David put his hands together and waved them. They looked like an egret flying up out of the marsh. Suddenly Ben leaped to his feet.

"It's the bay that matters!" he said, at the top of his voice. Then he quaked inside. The whole room was silent, looking at him, all grown-ups, except Matt. But he caught David Watchman's eye again, and

David smiled. "I don't care about the town growing or not growing," Ben went on. "But if the bay gets polluted to where the fish can't live, the oysters can't live, the birds can't live, then you've got no watermen. And if the marshes get filled up with a lot of stinking oil, there aren't going to be any tourists either. So you can have as many gas stations as you want, but *first* you've got to figure out where you're going to dump the old oil or the sewage or anything else that's bad for the bay. Because the bay is where we live." He sat down. The room was still silent. He wondered if he'd done a terrible thing, but Matt gave him the thumb's-up sign, and his father smiled proudly at him. Like a thunder clap, applause erupted from the room. Voices called out. "You tell 'em, Ben." "He's got that part right." "Atta boy."

Then many voices talked at once, and went on and on, until at last Matt made a sign and the two boys slipped out of the

161

church. They spent the rest of the evening throwing oyster shells at a stop sign, seeing who could hit the middle of the O. Finally people began coming out in twos and threes, but Ben's parents did not leave until almost the very end.

"Is it over?" asked Ben sleepily.

"No, Ben, I think it's just beginning," said his father.

13

The next day Ben was allowed to sleep late. By the time he got up, breakfast was finished and the house was empty. There weren't even any guests around. He decided the hot weather must have driven them all out to the ocean beaches, which were cooler and better for swimming. He found a note in the kitchen, saying that his mother and father had gone with Barbara and Eddie to church. After a quick bowl of cereal, Ben strolled down to the dock to see what was happening.

It was a bright morning and the water looked cool and blue. Another week or two of hot weather, and then school would be just around the corner. Ben would be in sixth grade, his last year in the elementary school. After that, he and Matt and the other kids from Marsh Harbor would take a bus to the next town, where the junior high school was. And then high school back here, and then . . . Ben thought about Eddie.

The water slapped against the dock, and the wooden pilings creaked and moaned. The crab shanties were empty this morning, and all the boats were at their moorings, with the morning sun on their white hulls. The arms that held the dredges bobbed up and down, up and down.

Ben sat perfectly still and watched an egret sail in, trailing its long legs. The big bird dipped, set its legs forward, and without a splash landed beside the dock in about three inches of water. It stood motionless, except for a tiny turning of its head, studying Ben's shape. The bird must have decided he was safe, for it turned to fishing.

"Ben Warren," he thought to himself. "That's my name. Warren, sounds like *warn.* I did that, I warned everyone that the station was dumping oil in the marsh. Me, Ben Warren."

The water slapped. A jellyfish floated under the dock. *Splash!* The egret swallowed a fish.

Ben stood up and walked slowly home. His parents were sitting at the table in the big kitchen, the late morning sun streaming through the white lace curtains. They were drinking coffee. His mother poured Ben a glass of orange juice.

He sat in his regular spot at the table. "Can you tell me about the meeting now?" he asked.

"Well," she began. "There were a lot of words, for the most part. But after a while, it seemed as if the most of the talk for growth was coming from a few outsiders. I won't say there's not some Marsh Harborans who want it, but mainly it's outsiders, real estate agents, builders like the fella that built the inn. But, the folks who live here, Ben, they agree with you about the bay. And that scientist fella, David Watchman, well, when he got up . . ."

"Did he talk? I knew he would!"

"He can talk, I guess," said Duke, taking over the story. "And he knows a few things. I respect a man who knows his business. Well, he told the meeting about what that oil dump would likely do to our part of the bay, and for how long, and what was going to be done about cleaning it up. It's bad, very bad, though that marsh is not dead yet. No sir, it's amazing what can be done, and the DNR is aiming to do it, and to make that gas station owner pay for it, too."

"Department of Natural Resources," Mary Warren whispered, and Ben smiled.

He was glad that the man he saw wasn't going to get all the punishment. After all, he thought, the guy's boss probably told him to do it. Not that that made it right. But the boss should get some of the punishment, too.

"So, to make a long story short," Duke went on, "what happened was, the mayor appointed a group of citizens to study what happens when Marsh Harbor expands. To find out, like, about the sewage. Or where to dump stuff. Or if they built parking lots, would a lot of pollutants be running into the marshes. Questions like that."

"But won't that take a long time?"

Duke nodded. "Might take a long time. But it's the only way. Because you can't just give up and let the bay die. That's not the way."

"But what if they build more inns and motels and restaurants and stores in the meantime?"

"They can't," said his mother. "No more construction until we find a safe way. That's the town's decision."

"Wow." Ben thought about it. "Can you build the new wing?" he asked.

"I don't know for sure," she said. "It'll take some time to find out if the sewage system we have can handle it. And if it's not right, we'll have to wait to do it. Your dad will help check that out."

Ben was confused.

"I am part of the mayor's new committee," Duke Warren explained, smiling. "Who knows, maybe I'll go up to Annapolis and ask for a few more regulations down here. Because someday, I want my son to be a waterman on the Chesapeake Bay."

Ben laughed and threw his arms around his father.

"You coming out on the water with me again tomorrow, Ben? I sure could use some help. Oyster season's coming up, and we've got to catch crabs while we can."

"I'm coming, Dad." Ben felt so happy he wanted to jump around the kitchen, but he thought he was too old for that.

"But, Dad."

"Yes?"

"I might not want to be a waterman."

"Oh?" Duke's eyebrows shot up with surprise and Mary set down her cup.

"Yeah, because"—Ben squirmed a little—"well, I was thinking about college. Eddie says he likes it. And David Watchman went to college, but he still spends lots of time on the water. And I'm kind of interested, you know." Ben stopped. He didn't know what he wanted or how to talk about it.

"You want to be a scientist, like Mr. Watchman?" asked Duke.

169

"Well, I *might*."

"Could do worse." Duke Warren laughed and stood up. Picking his son up by the waist, he twirled him around in the air, like he used to do when Ben was a little boy.

"Aagh! Dad, put me down!"

Duke laughed. Setting Ben on his feet, he kissed his wife and said, "Got to get down to the shanty. Got some softshells that need pulling."

"Can I go over to Matt's, then?" asked Ben.

"Go along with you both," said Mary Warren. "I've got six guests due in tonight. Next thing you know Barbara will be applying to college too, so we'd best be making money. And you, Ben, don't go exploring in any more oily marshes. Or I'll put you in charge of the laundry."

"Right, Mom." The screen door banged, and in half a minute Ben was peeling around the corner past the Dari Dreme.

Glossary

al·gae (al´ jē) *n.* A group of simple plants with no roots, stems, or leaves that grow in water. *Sometimes, algae in the pond look like green scum.*

ca·pac·i·ty (kə pas´ i tē) *n.* An amount of space that can be filled. *The small tank has a capacity of only one gallon.*

caulk (kôk) *n.* A soft, pasty substance used to fill in cracks. *They put caulk around the windows so the wind wouldn't get in.*

con·tam·i·nant (kən tam´ ə nənt) *n.* A substance that contaminates or pollutes another substance such as air or water. *After experimenting with the sea water, they discover that the contaminant is dishwashing soap.*

con·tra·dic·to·ry (kän trə dik´ tə rē) *adj.* Saying the opposite. *The policeman couldn't decide who caused the accident because the drivers' stories were contradictory.*

co·pe·pod (kō´ pə pod) *n.* A kind of tiny, hard-shelled animal living in fresh or salt water. *The copepod is an important food for sea animals.*

cul·prit (kul´ prit) *n.* A person guilty of a crime. *He is the culprit who pours garbage into the lake.*

de·bris (də brē´) *n.* The scattered remains of broken and torn objects, trash, or garbage. *They wear gloves when they pick up the debris on the beach.*

leach (lēch) *v.* To dissolve and soak into the surrounding area. *The camper's dishwashing soap is leaching into the lake.*

marsh (märsh) *n.* A low land that is soft and wet. *A marsh can have tall weeds.*

mo·rose (mə rōs´) *adj.* Feeling down or gloomy. *She feels tired and morose because it's raining, and she has nothing to do.*

plank·ton (plank´ tən) *n.* A combination of tiny plants and animals found floating in water. *They place the plankton under a microscope so that they can see all the tiny water life.*

scow (skou) *n.* A large, flat-bottom boat used for carrying heavy loads. *To move people to the island, movers use a scow.*

si·dle (sī´ dəl) *v.* To move sideways. *Crabs moving across the sand look funny as they sidle.*

smug (smug) *adj.* Appearing to be very pleased with oneself because of knowing something. *The others dislike his smug looks when he knows answers they don't know.*

spawn (spôn) *v.* To produce eggs in large numbers. *Saltwater fish such as salmon move into freshwater streams to spawn.*

spec·ter (spek´ tər) *n.* The ghost or imaginary presence of someone who is troublesome. *The people at the town meeting shouted, not so much at each other, but at the specter of the corrupt mayor.*

squall (skwôl) *n.* A violent windstorm that comes up suddenly and just as suddenly disappears. *A squall is especially dangerous for small boats on the water.*

sub·merge (sub mʉrj´) *v.* To cover with water. *The plant store owners submerge all their flower pots in tanks of water.*

wat·er·man (wôt´ ər mən) *n.* The name for a person who makes his living on the water, often by fishing. *Although the family lives by the sea, only the uncle is a waterman with a lobster boat.*